Nerd Gangs of New York

MJ Buck

Published by Mix'd Books, 2023.

NERD GANGS OF NEW YORK

First edition. September 30, 2023.

Copyright © 2023 MJ Buck.

ISBN: 978-0982469613

Written by MJ Buck.

This book has been influenced by:

J Michael Straczynski's series Babylon 5 with the introduction of the Techno Mages

Arthur C. Clarke's 3rd Law defined in his 1962 book, "Profiles of the Future: An Inquiry into the Limits of the Possible". For those who have forgotten his laws they are:

- When a distinguished but elderly scientist states that something is possible, he is almost certainly right. When he states that something is impossible, he is very probably wrong,

- The only way of discovering the limits of the possible is to venture a little way past them into the impossible.

- Any sufficiently advanced technology is indistinguishable from magic.

CHAPTER 1

There was a time when the street gangs in New York were the subject of fear and loathing.
Shunned or outright exterminated if you could find a way. But that was many years ago.

The SPIDRs changed everything. If it hadn't been for the SPIDRs, the three of us probably wouldn't have ended up creating the most successful and lucrative street gang in New York City. I might not even be around right now if it hadn't been for them. Short, skinny, and brilliant is not a safe combination in any high school, no matter what city you live in; but when your high school is also surrounded by turfs held by three different street gangs...your focus tends to dwindle down to pure survival. Survival that depended heavily on my ability to stay off the local gang's radar.

The path from Thomas Jefferson Public High School to the third-floor walkup where I lived ran right through the turf owned by the NEG. I could have gone around their zone, if I wanted to walk five city blocks up and back, but their turf was only two blocks deep, while it was 9 blocks long. I had pretty well scoped them out and knew exactly where most of them hung, so I usually could slip past. It helped a lot that I generally hung out at the school library until late, so that the sun was down, or nearly so. It made avoiding the bullies on the school property easier since they tended to escape the place as fast as they could at the end of the day. By the time I headed out, they were usually long gone. The days when they hung around were usually right before term papers or other major assignments were due. Which was OK since I made a nice profit doing their homework and writing term papers for them. Most of them weren't dumb enough to damage their best source for a passing grade.

Twilight was closing in fast as I slipped from one shadowed doorway to the next, avoiding the working girls on the corner as they tried to attract some business. Around the corner then cut through St. Peter the Redeemer Catholic church. I nodded to Father Anthony as I crossed between the pews and out the side door near the nave. I was probably disrespectful to cut through every evening but Father Anthony didn't mind as long as I didn't do it during mass. I had done that once and the next day he had caught me and held me a long time while he delivered a lecture on respect for the church and disrespect for God. He didn't come down on me too hard though, he knows what kind of neighborhood the church sits in and knows that it's one of the few relatively safe places on the NEG turf.

I raised one hand in a semi-wave as I passed through and he nodded in response, his hands full of fresh candles and his bald head shining softly in the flickering light. Out the side door and onto the sidewalk of sixth street. I paused to take a deep breath, savoring the sensation of one more safe trip home. Well, not quite home, but at least through the NEG zone.

Half a block up and I slid sideways into the recessed doorway to the Heavenly Delights Deli, sniffing the air appreciatively. Carla's dad must have been making his special Korean

Ddonkkaseu Kimbap (who doesn't like fried pork?). The smells leaking out through the doorway were enough to make your stomach growl and your mouth water. The Heavenly Delights Deli is my second favorite place to hang out, right up there behind the computer lab at school. Mr. Pak had brought the family to the United States when he was in his twenties and the deli was his pride and joy. Well, to be honest, his daughter Carla held that title, but the deli was a close second.

When I stepped inside Mr. Pak was in the back, raving in Korean. I couldn't understand most of what he was yelling but it was clear that something was seriously wrong. I sidled up to the counter and looked at Carla.

"What's going on?"

Carla Pak was one of the prettiest girls I knew, but totally unconscious of the effect she had on the guys around her. Having a Korean father and Puerto Rican mother had given her long, blue-black hair that curled just above her hips, green eyes with just a hint of a tilt at the corners, and skin the color of warm caramel. She glanced towards the back room and frowned, worried lines forming between her arched brows. One hand waved at the cash register.

"We got robbed...again. A couple of toughs from the NEG came in and cleared out the register. They took a bunch of food as well". Her scowl deepened as Mr. Pak's voice rose another octave higher. "As they left, they took the time to beat the crap out of Joey".

Joey was a teenager who worked after school at the deli. He covered the counter so that Mr. Pak could prepare the dinner menu. At six foot two, he wasn't a usual target for bullies and gangbangers and I wondered what he had done to provoke them.

"Why'd they do that, any idea?"

"The cops think that the NEG is planning an expansion in our direction. Dad is so upset that he is talking about closing the deli and moving away".

Businesses like the Heavenly Delights Deli got robbed with a certain regularity but most of the time it was just punks shoplifting. After all, other than the cash, it isn't like you could sell or spend stolen noodles. I looked at the back room again and thought about what had happened.

Part of the problem was that people like Mr. Pak generally don't really want to go to court and testify against gang members. The occasional problem just wasn't worth the trouble that you would attract if you pressed charges against members of any gang. Those guys got riled up fast and any official action taken against them would probably put Carla and Maria Pak, Carla's mother, at risk. With her looks, Carla was at risk in this neighborhood anyway but why invite trouble?

"There must be something that can be done to stop those guys. Why don't the police do something?" She always called them the police, never cops or any of the other pejoratives that people have come up with for law enforcement over the years.

"Think for a second Carla", I countered. "If your dad identifies the two guys who robbed the deli and beat up Joey, and if they really are NEG, what would the rest of the gang do? More than likely they would be here in force, probably tear the place apart, maybe even kill your dad, or worse..". I took a deep breath before continuing. "You could find yourself the victim of a gang rape as a way to punish your father for getting their members in trouble".

She huffed a loud breath and crossed her arms over her chest, looking annoyed rather than scared. "Well there must be some way to stop them! Why don't you think of something?"

"Whoa, how did solving crime and social injustice become my job?"

"Aren't you the one with the IQ of 196? All those brains and you can't find a solution?"

Now that was patently unfair. Yeah, I have an intelligence quotient that's pretty much off the Richter scale, but Carla is no slouch either. I had hacked her school records a couple of years back and knew that she was pretty well up in the genius range. Not quite as high as me, but pretty darn respectable just the same. In fact, there was only one other person in the twenty-five hundred students at Thomas Jefferson High School who beat her score. I thought about that for a moment and the core of an idea began to form in my brain.

"Listen Carla, tell your dad not to do anything precipitous. I think I may have an idea". My brain was rapidly kicking into overdrive, so I stumbled a bit over the words. "Can you get your dad to calm down and give us some time? I need to talk to Q and then we need to get together and work a few things out. Meet us at the library in the morning before first period".

She stared at me for a long moment before answering, "I didn't really expect you to solve this, you know".

"Yeah, I know. But I think I might be onto a solution. Meet me in the morning?" I was already edging towards the door, eager to get home and think things through.

"Sure". She didn't look sure but I wasn't about to argue the point.

"Great, see you then".

The bell jangled as I yanked open the door and nearly ran into a customer on his way in.

I DIDN'T GET MUCH SLEEP that night. I spent most of it in front of my computer working out details and putting together some truly epic code. The machine was an old laptop that the school had retired a year earlier. I had snagged it when they set it aside for recycling. It was old, slow, and weighed about half a ton, but it ran...and the price (free) had been right.

By the time dawn rolled in, I was bleary with fatigue but at the same time so stoked on adrenaline that I felt like I could stay awake for a week. I dressed in the dark, grabbed some toast and was out the door before the sun was completely up.

I did stop to write a note to my mom before I left. She worried a lot about me growing up so near gang territory and I didn't want to add to her fears by having her wonder where I had gone.

Mom,

I have an early study session with Q and Carla. Physics exam tomorrow (which was true) and they need the extra help (which wasn't true). Back by the usual time.

Love Harold

I never used Harold except when dealing with mom. Being saddled with a name like that, when you're skinny, short, brainy, and wear glasses is just too much of a stereotype for me to handle.

Most of the time people called me Mouse. Carla and Quentin ("Q") both just called me "H" and left it at that. I appreciated their discretion.

I slipped out the front door, closing it as quietly as I could, and headed down the stairs. The Raines twins were a few steps ahead of me and I tried to ignore their chatter as they ambled down the narrow stairwell. My brain was overflowing, and I really hated listening to them chatter about clothes and boys...or boys and clothes, depending on the day of the week. I ran into Q as soon as I reached the sidewalk.

Q is a full foot taller than me, which makes him well above average height. He's also pretty much my opposite in every way. Tall, with a muscular build and skin like a shadow at twilight. Where my hair is mousey brown and longish, he keeps his as about a quarter of an inch of lamb's wool. He's ebony to my ivory and we had been best friends since the third grade. He is also one of the best pure engineers you will ever see. While I build software code, I had never seen any gizmo he couldn't either build from scratch or fix, even without schematics.

He had been "Q" ever since we saw our first James Bond flick. I knew that most people thought that being a science nerd, Q had to be for the Star Trek character but his ultimate hero was actually MI-6's quintessential British genius Q, he of the invisible cars, exploding chewing gum, and laser watches.

He grinned at me. "Hey, I got your email. Sucks about Mr. Pak and what happened to Joey. I assume you have a plan?"

CHAPTER 2

The best laid plans
         I knew I probably looked like hell and Carla didn't look much better. I assumed that things in her house hadn't gotten much better overnight and she was worried that her dad would pull the plug before we could do anything significant enough to make a difference.

"So, what's up H? You have a plan or what?" Q, by contrast, was unreasonably fresh and way too chipper for the hour but I did have a plan, or at least the start of one, so I let it pass.

"Yeah, I have a couple of ideas. Gonna need both of you to help flesh them out though".

"Excellent!" He rubbed his hands together like a used car salesman scenting a deal in the wind.

"So quit stalling and give us the details already".

We had picked out a table way in the back of the library's main reading room where we could spread out and talk. I eased myself down into a chair and sighed heavily, wishing I had stopped for coffee before getting to the library. A double espresso sounded about right based on my sleep deprived state.

"So, I think we can all agree that the NEG is making a move to annex our street and bring it into their own turf, right?"

The two of them nodded so I continued. "What I think is needed is a way to slow or stop them...stop by preference before they get any further into our area.

Carla scowled at me, "so tell us something we don't already know...like how you think the three of us can have any affect at all on that crew. I don't know about you guys, but I'm pretty sure they aren't going to be scared by three uncool teenage brains".

That got a grin from me. "Actually, I think they are going to learn to fear us, even if they don't know who is coming after them". I looked back and forth between them, "That's the real trick, to shut them down without bringing their attention onto

us or our families. Right?"

"Neat trick if you can manage it. I don't think I have ever heard of anybody who has come up with something that will stop a gang in it is tracks that way".

Q paused and then continued; his head tipped to one side as if he was dredging up an old, old memory. "Well, maybe the Guardian Angels managed it, for a while. But even they couldn't make it stick and they had a lot more than just three members".

"Sure, but they tried to fight fire with fire. I plan to fight it with science".

"Enough foreplay H, just tell us what you have in mind". Carla's comment hung in the air for a moment and then she turned red when she realized exactly what she had said. "Oh...you know what I mean.

Watching her get flustered was interesting. Usually she was so calm and imperturbable that the blush made her look about fourteen. I grinned and finally took pity on her.

"OK, What I have in mind is a plan that takes part in several stages". I pulled out a sheet of paper with my notes from the previous night and started to read down the list".

"1: We need to seriously beef up security at the deli. Not just new cameras, but some serious controls and evidence collection tools to provide solid intel to the cops...when the time is right".

"2: We need to get surveillance into the NEG ranks".

That comment drew a gasp from Carla and wide-eyed incredulity from both of them. "Are you crazy? You want us to infiltrate the NEG?" Carla was nearly shouting.

Q's response was a bit softer but several levels of sarcasm deeper, "So you planning to go all

James Bond on us? Somehow I don't think you're cut out for the role".

I smiled at them, my calm making them both even more nervous.

"More Q than James actually".

"Me!" His voice cracked, "oh wait...the other "Q"".

Personally, as dangerous as what I planned was, I was having fun making them work for the information and waiting to see how long it would take for them to figure things out. I didn't often get to get the better of the two of them and I was milking the moment for all it was worth.

"Think about it. These guys are punks. High school dropouts and more brawn than brains. Well, most of them. There must be a couple of brighter ones in the crowd holding the whole thing together and guiding the money-making portions of their activities. Even so, I don't think they can beat out our combined brain power. We just need to out science them a bit".

"A bit?"

"Well, ok, a lot. But I don't think it's beyond us. I have a few ideas.

PHASE ONE WAS RELATIVELY straight forward. At least on the surface it seemed that way. Upgrade security at the Heavenly Delights Deli so that they could have better surveillance and be able to provide iron clad evidence to the cops.

It was a total shame that it didn't go as smoothly as it seemed up front. First, we had to convince Mr. Pak that we wouldn't take the evidence to the cops until (unless) we had the NEG on the ropes, and he was far less likely to suffer retaliation from them.

The next hurdle was to design some brand-new equipment and software to run the new system. Now, you might be wondering how three kids from Queens, with only a public-school education would know how to do any of this. What most people don't realize is that a few years back, bowing to the inevitable pressures of the information age and the internet, the world's best universities and colleges started putting every one of their courses online...for free. Want to learn engineering? Log on and do the entire engineering curriculum at MIT. Interested in programming in Fortran, or Cobol, or any other language out there? Try out the courses at Stanford. The amazing thing is that these aren't sample courses, they are the same ones that people pay megabucks to take as full-time students. There is only one difference, you don't get credit when you take the course for free. Honestly though, if all you want is to learn and you don't really care about earning college credit or a degree, then you can learn pretty much any subject on your own, for nothing except the effort it itself. I thought it was pretty sweet and had already finished enough courses for a solid Masters in poly-sci. Carla and Q weren't very far behind in the number and variety of classes they had completed. They just chose different subjects.

Between us we had an extensive footing in software development, mechanical engineering, robotics, and business management disciplines. I figured we could handle just about anything that we could dream up.

We spent the next week redesigning Mr. Pak's cash register using the manufacturer's tech manuals (available from the company online). Q re-worked the cash drawer to use a bill scanner we scavenged from a dead soda machine. I reworked the software for the scanner so that it could identify any size bill, up to hundreds. Carla installed a miniature camera and fiber optic light so that the system could take and store images of the bills as they were put in and removed. We also modified the drawer so that mechanical arms removed any bills over a set limit and stored them deeper in the belly of the register. The end effect was that the cash drawer visible when you opened it would never contain more than a pre-determined amount of money. Even if the deli got robbed again, they would never get very much.

I would have liked to claim full credit for the revised software but I ended up using a piece of code I hacked from the servers at BEC (I call them Big Evil Corporation). Of course, that isn't the company's real name, but I have no desire to get sued so I'll just use that as a pseudonym for them. They had been airing splashy ads for about a month touting their new, breakthrough Artificial Intelligence system and I had been hacking them almost since day one. I had to admit that their new system was sweet and I was suffering from a fair amount of professional jealousy over it. It was a point of pride that I was able to hack it repeatedly, even though it had bleeding edge security protocols. I wasn't sure how they did it, but the system learned FAST. It was a pleasant challenge to stay ahead of it. Anyway, I used a chunk of code I swiped from them to finish the bill scanning system and it ran smooth as honey. The whole setup was a thing of beauty.

It took Carla most of the week to convince her father to let us operate on his beloved cash register. I think he expected it to blow up when we were done with it. The three of us tore it down and rebuilt it by staying up all night on Saturday then had to spend most of Sunday helping each other to teach him about the changes.

"Why two keys to open the drawer when I only needed one key before?"

I sighed inwardly and started again. "If you only use one key, the "no sale" key, then the security system will activate. No alarm but it starts all the cameras and records what money is taken out as well as taking video of the whole store until the drawer is closed".

It was the third or fourth time I had run through the drill with him but he just didn't seem to be getting it.

"So, one key alone means you're being robbed. Two keys, the No Sale key and the Total key together means you just want to take money out, for example at the end of the day to count it".

Carla interrupted me, firing off a long spate of Korean at him. I had no idea what she was saying but from her face and body language I guessed that she was angry with him. He answered and she nearly shouted at him, her arms windmilling for emphasis about...something.

"Okay, Okay". He turned to me. "Dinner now Harold? Sundubu-jjigae?"

My mouth watered. The spicy stew made with soft tofu was one of my favorites and he knew it.

"Sure Mr. Pak, that sounds great".

Carla scowled and tossed one hand in the air, "men!" She rounded on me, "What about the rest of it HAROLD, you gonna explain that too or is it supposed to be my job?"

CHAPTER 3

L et the spy games begin
       We lost a couple of days at that point because Toby Grey overdosed in the middle of school and everyone had to attend a whole series of drug awareness sessions that ate up all our free periods. I was surprised because Toby didn't seem to the be type to screw around with drugs. He was another habitual honor student and although he wasn't a particular friend of ours, we saw enough of him in some of the advanced placement classes to get a feel for his personality.

"Just goes to show that everyone has secrets, I guess".

Carla wasn't really buying that unfortunately and she kept harping on the fact that Toby had been a vegan and kept trying to convince everybody in his vicinity to avoid GMOs (genetically modified foods). I had to agree that the idea of him taking drugs was a bit out of character.

"Maybe somebody slipped something into his water bottle when he wasn't paying attention. Or maybe the whole health food, vegan thing was a cover. Who knows?

Q sauntered up to the library table where we were sitting and spun a chair around, straddling it with his arms crossed on top of the seat back. "Talking about Toby?"

"Yeah, it's just so weird and the good Lord knows I'm tired of hearing the counselors with their anti-drug shtick. You'd figure they would know that if we hadn't been paying attention to this point, they probably aren't going to make a difference now".

Carla scowled, "don't be so sure. I hear he's in a coma and they can't figure out why. His girlfriend is freaking out".

"Whatever". Q waved a hand in dismissal. "I have a new idea on data gathering if you two of you're done gossiping like a couple of old biddies".

I threw my pen at his head but he ducked out of the line of fire. The pen clattered to the faded linoleum floor and Ms. Pinchely; the librarian scowled in our direction. I mouthed "sorry" and scooped it off the floor, slipping it back into my shirt pocket.

"So, what's this great new brainstorm of yours?" Carla was leaning back in her chair, lips pursed and looking down her nose at us for our antics. I never have figured out how she does that, when she is so much shorter than either of us guys.

"SPIDRs". His voice was a triumphant whisper.

"Eew, spiders?" Her nose wrinkled in disgust. "What do you have in mind...tarantulas with little microphones strapped to their backs?"

"Oh, Ha...Ha.. No, not spider...S.P.I.D.R".

I leaned forward a bit further, "So what the heck is a SPIDR then".

"Surveillance Probe Independent Data Relay".

Even Carla was starting to show some interest by that point.

Q reached into his shirt pocket and pulled out a miniscule plastic box, sitting it gently in the middle of the table. Neither Carla nor I moved, we just sat and stared back and forth from Q to the little cube. After savoring being the center of attention for a long moment, he reached out and flipped open the cover. Inside sat what looked like a small object with six legs and a round body. It really did look kind of like a medium sized spider, except that I had never seen a spider with a shiny metal body before.

I picked up the box gingerly and brought it close to my face, trying to make out more details. The body was about the size of the fingernail on my pinkie finger and the legs, if that's what they were, were evenly spaced, three to a side and about the thickness of a couple of human hairs. The legs reminded me mostly of stubby cat whiskers.

Carla was holding her hand out, palm up, and I put the box into it then looked back at Q.

"So... what does it do?"

"Well...once you create the software for it, it will collect both sound and picture, transmit them back to its Momma, and she'll send it on to me". He leaned over and retrieved it, smiling down at it like a proud papa. Which I suppose he was, in a way.

Then I realized what he had said.

"Wait, you mean it doesn't do anything?"

"Yet, grasshopper. It doesn't do anything YET. But no, that isn't accurate. Right now, the camera works and so does the mic. It's capable of transmitting what it sees. It just doesn't know where to go and when to start transmitting, or even what frequency to use. I built this beauty, but programming is your job".

I stared for a long moment. Too long apparently because Carla interrupted and brought me out of my mental tailspin, "Can you do it H? Can you program this little critter to do what Q is saying it can?

"Maybe". I looked back at Q, "What exactly do I need to program it to do, and how much memory do I have to work with?"

Carla broke in, "And just how to you plan to deploy this thing so that it can do all this? What is it is effective range for sound pickup? How far can it move on it is own...or can it move on its own at all? What's the resolution of the camera? What is the battery life?"

She paused to take a breath and I jumped back into the conversation, "For that matter, what is the power source? I can't imagine that it would last very long, considering the size of the thing".

"Would you believe me if I told you it doesn't have a power source?"

"Sure I would. But that would mean that it's basically a pretty toy and not capable of doing anything except sit there and be shiny".

Q laughed, "Perhaps I should have said that it doesn't have any onboard power source".

"That makes even less sense. If it doesn't have any internal power, it can't do anything".

"Fat lot you know". H paused for dramatic effect and then said, very softly so that his voice didn't reach the next table, "It harvests ambient energy from its environment".

I STARED. HE MIGHT as well have said that the thing used cold fusion for all the sense his answer made. Carla recovered first.

"Ambient power. From light or random current frequencies?"

He cocked his index finger at her as if it were a gun and said, "Got it in one bright girl".

I was annoyed. Q always did that, dropped some enigmatic idea into the conversation just to see who would catch on first. I understood both concepts for power generation but didn't see any way to fit either one into something as small as the SPIDR.

"Which one?" was all I said.

He tilted his nose down, as if he were looking at me over the rim of invisible glasses, which he didn't wear, and clipped out. "Do try to keep up H".

Even I had to laugh at that; he had Q's line down cold including the annoyed British condescension. Not John Cleese's Q from the most recent movie but the earlier Desmond Llewellyn classic Q.

"Of course". I picked up the box with the tiny critter in it and he snatched it out of my hand.

"And TRY not to break anything".

Then he laughed and handed it back.

"So, how does it work?"

"I got most of the design from thinking about every spy movie I have ever seen. What do they almost all have?"

"Gorgeous, scantily clad women?"

"Aside from that you idiot". He waited but when neither of us answered, he continued, "tiny surveillance systems. Cameras and communications equipment built into eyeglasses, tie tacks, cufflinks, and so on. Generally, all providing full sound and video".

I thought about it for a long moment. He was right. Most spy movies either relied on violence or high tech to gather intelligence information. Some, like the James Bond series, balanced the two. In fact, for Bond stories it was almost obligatory for Q to come up with several cool new tech toys for James to play with. From invisible cars, to exploding pens, and watches with lasers included. Not to mention the myriad of spy movies that had the hero wearing glasses that provided full surveillance feeds back to some poor slob hunched in the back of a van one block down the street. That guy was always feeding information back to the hero, identifying people, or giving directions to the secret panel that hides the safe.

"So, you built a surveillance bug. Fine. You still haven't explained your ambient power solution to us".

He settled deeper in his chair as if he was preparing to be there for a long time and needed to get comfortable first.

"Right. So, you know that every electronic device, and even the power lines leak a bit, right?"

"Sure. That's why people out in the western states complain so much about all those huge power line towers running through the countryside. They claim that the power leakage on those things is so bad that it's causing health problems for the families that live under them. But we don't have those here. There're also all those nut cases who claim that the leakage from cell phones causes brain cancer".

"Exactly! Most of the time the leakage is so tiny that you couldn't measure it with a standard voltmeter. But that doesn't mean it isn't there...because it is. It's everywhere. Especially here in the city. Do you have any idea how many electronic devices there are within a single city block? Think about it for a moment. Not just cell phones but television, computers, tablets, refrigerators, stoves, air conditioners, hair dryers, curling irons, toasters". He paused for breath, "the list is staggering. AND every single one of those things leaks a little bit of energy".

I stared at him. "My God, you found a way to tap into that?"

CHAPTER 4

I nvasion of the SPIDRs

It took me almost a month to finish the programming for the SPIDR. Q's solution for power was incredible but the memory in each unit was limited so I had to resort to some fancy dancing to get the coding to be efficient enough to load in them. He spent the time making more of them and by the end of the month, we had a couple of dozen available to deploy against the NEG.

I must admit, Carla did a nice job on camouflaging them. The prototype that Q had shown us was brilliantly metallic and anybody who looked at it would have instantly realized that it wasn't a real insect. She had painted them with flat enamel paints that she filched from her little brother's model car stuff. Using brushes that were hardly more than a single hair thick, she hand painted the body and legs of each SPIDR to cover their metal skin and help them blend into their surroundings.

The things were incredible, and I spent a whole day at Qs house watching him assemble one from parts that he either made himself or "borrowed" from his part time job at a local phone repair shop. People were always bringing in phones that were pretty much dead and he either repaired them or sold them a refurbished unit if theirs was too far gone. The truly dead ones were supposed to get recycled but he kept a lot of them for himself, claiming that he was recycling them, just not the way everybody thought of the process.

He also made a couple of larger units that he called the mama SPIDRs. The tiny ones would be able to get into a lot of places and go unnoticed for the most part but they didn't have a lot of range for

19

their transmissions. The mother SPIDR would be stationed someplace nearby and act as a relay station for up to three babies.

My favorite was one of the mother SPIDRs. When Carla got done with it, the thing was gorgeous. It had a body about the size of a nickel but oval shaped, painted matte black with a round white patch on the back. The head was about half that size and a pearly gray. In fact it was about the size of a pearl and that shiny grayish color you see on black pearls. The legs were long and delicate, with bands of red and gray. The overall effect was of an oversized daddy long-legs decked out for Mardi gras but I thought it was beautiful.

"I patterned it after pictures of hurricane SPIDRs that I found online. Although they're usually more yellow or orange than red. Still, she is pretty, isn't she?" She grinned in enthusiasm.

"Amazing. Not sure how well she'll hide but she sure is pretty".

"Oh, the colors almost disappear when she is in deep shadow". She cupped her hands over the thing to help demonstrate. "It's just the light in here that makes her look so bright".

IN THE END, I HAD TO go back to the BEC AI to finish the software. I probably could have done it myself, given enough time. But I was under pressure from the others to get it finished so that the SPIDRs could be deployed.

BEC. Inc. was still advertising the heck out of their new AI and I thought it was silly that they mostly had the thing saying hello to people and demonstrating simple conversation skills. I could have built a program to do the same stuff without claiming that the program had any intelligence. The task probably wouldn't have taken much more than a weekend. The ads didn't seem to prove anything. Especially once I had hacked the system and spent some time "talking" with it. It was more like talking to a friend than a machine. I found myself discussing in plain language what I was trying to accomplish and where I was stuck. I explained the problem and the AI came up with some slick recommendations on ways to make things better.

It wasn't at all like doing an online search. You know what I mean. "What restaurants are nearby" and the system comes back with stock phrase answers like "I found the following restaurants near your location".

I took to calling it RALPH for some reason that I didn't want to examine too closely. I guess we all tend to animism when it comes to machines sometimes.

Anyway, I could just talk to RALPH.

"Hey RALPH, I'm having a hard time figuring out a better way to reduce the size of the code in section 42 of the communications package we discussed yesterday".

RALPH: "Hmm, let me look. Have you considered what would happen if you...?

You get the idea. It was like talking to a real person buy their advertising idiots had the thing saying "Hello" and "I'm pleased to meet you" to famous people on TV. It made me wonder about their media department's competence.

Anyway, I didn't get much sleep that month and I was dragging through all my classes. A couple of teachers asked me if everything was alright at home while both Carla and Q kept asking if I was OK all the time. I reassured the teachers but I'm not very proud of how I responded to my friends.

"No, I'm not all right! I'm exhausted, I can't get the stupid GPS package to load and the communications software has developed a bug that makes it crash every time the Mama SPIDR

tries to relay".

Q looked hurt but Carla just took my arm and started walking towards the door. "C'mon, you need to get out of this apartment and get some down time".

"But..". I tried to pull my arm away but she had a grip on my wrist that was like being dragged by the Terminator.

"No buts. You come with us, NOW".

They hauled me out for tacos and we sat on the bench at a bus stop while they talked about anything and everything except the project.

"The doctors say Toby isn't going to wake up".

I stared at Carla, "what?"

"Toby, Toby Grey? Remember how he overdosed last month? He's still in a coma and the doctor's say he probably won't ever wake up. They've moved him out of St. Thomas Hospital to some research center in Flatbush".

"Wow". It was all I could think to say.

"Yeah", she sighed. "His parents aren't really very happy about him being moved but they can't afford to keep him at St. Thomas and the research facility specializes in coma patients. A government grant or something pays for everything".

"Well, maybe they'll find an answer. They probably know more about what causes comas than the general medicine doctors here in Queens would".

She looked thoughtful. "True. His parents thought they were going to have to decide whether to pull the plug or not when this research group offered to take over his care".

Both Q and I shifted uncomfortably at this. His older brother had been mugged and ended up brain dead a few years back. His parents had made that same choice so the situation with Toby really struck home for him.

"That sucks", was all he said.

"How did you learn all this Carla?"

"His girlfriend lives in my building. We talk sometimes and I found her crying this morning. She told me the whole thing".

"That sucks", Q repeated.

We sat around for a few minutes, feeling uniformly morose, when he suddenly popped to his feet. "Let's go. I feel the need to be in motion".

When I got back home I headed straight to my computer.

There was a message alert on the screen.

Try this... RALPH.

When I clicked on the attached file, a short string of code filled the resulting pop-up window. It was sublime. Elegant and simple, the offered code fixed my communications issue by looping through a whole different path in a way I had never seen before, not from any programmer, ever.

I scrolled through it three time and then hit reply. **Thanks RALPH, you're a genius. H**

A moment later another alert popped up. I know...LOL. RALPH

I stared at it. LOL? The artificial Intelligence was Laughing Out Loud? I snorted in derision yet again at the BEC advertising morons then settled in to get some work done.

With RALPH's help I managed to finish all the software fixes by late the next morning. Thank God it was Saturday and I could crash without worrying about trying to drag my sorry butt across NEG territory to school.

CHAPTER 5

S PIDR Attack
We put the SPIDRs through their paces the next day with Q playing the part of a punk robbing the Heavenly Delights Deli. It was a disaster.

The plan had been for a SPIDR to be dropped onto a gang member when the No Sale key was pushed on the cash register. It sounded cool but we quickly realized that there were a bunch of problems with the plan. First, we had no way to aim them when they were dropped from the ceiling. More often than not they landed on the floor next to Q's foot and in danger of being stepped on, just like a real spider. When they did land on him, he always felt it. It wasn't much of a leap to figure out that if somebody felt something unexpected land on their head or shoulder, they were probably going to try to brush it off. The SPIDR would end up back on the floor again.

We had discussed having them ride the NEG members back to their hangout from the time of the robbery but soon realized that the plan wasn't viable. We were going to have to find another way to deploy them and get them back to where they could observe the gang and transmit back to us.

"Look", I said. "Why don't we just deploy them directly into the NEG territory. We know who most of those guys are. Brush up against one of their associates at school and plant one of the babies on it. Then we use Mama SPIDR to track the baby".

"You volunteering to be the bait for that? Most of those guys are likely to pound you for bumping into them".

"Make them into a pair of earrings". We turned to stare at Carla, who was grinning.

"Earrings...really? What good would that do?

"I know one of the girls who got jumped into the NEG last spring. She's a total idiot but she likes to pretend she's tough. Has a thing for goth jewelry and a spiderweb tattoo high up on the left side of her chest, where the edge peeks out from her neckline most of the time".

My sarcasm got the better of me, unfortunately. "So, what? You going to walk up to her and give them to her as a present?"

She rolled her eyes and sneered at me. "Of course not. But if I wear them and get anywhere near her, she won't be able to resist them. She'll demand that I give them to her. I'll refuse. She'll threaten to beat me up or else if I don't hand them over". She made air quotes when she said "or else".

She leaned back and raised both hands with her palms out, as if pleading for her life.

"After being suitably cowed by her big, bad, gangsta threats; I'll meekly hand the earrings over to avoid getting pounded into the dirt. I slink away and she puts the earrings on in triumph. Then she walks right into their hangout wearing them and giving us exactly the intel that we need".

I had to admit it, her plan did seem plausible. We argued with her a bit, just to maintain form. But eventually we gave in and did it her way. We did have to get Q to modify the earring bugs to have their lenses on the SPIDR's back instead of where a real spider's eyes would normally be. Otherwise we'd never have seen much other than her shoulders or cleavage...although that had its own merits as plans go.

THE EARRING CAPER ALMOST went off without a hitch except that the first day Carla tried it, the girl she was aiming for wasn't at school. The target was a pale chick with long straight black hair, brown eyes, and heavy dark eye makeup, who went by the seriously unlikely nickname of Arika.

I mean, c'mon the name sounds like it belongs to some blonde-haired blue-eyed valley girl, not a goth chic from Queens. For my money, considering that she wasn't exactly a petite female, she looked more like a Brunhilda than an Arika. But then, I didn't choose the name for her so I guess my opinion really doesn't mean much, under the circumstances.

In the end, she had to wear the earrings for almost a week before she ran into Arika. When they finally did cross paths, the scene went down exactly the way she had described it, almost word for word.

"There was a reason that I did all those online psych and sociology classes from Stanford", was all she said after it was over.

The three of us were sitting in my bedroom with the hallway door standing part of the way open. It was a rule my mom had put in place years ago, when I showed the first signs of noticing that girls were different from boys. No girls in my room unless the door stayed open. Mom was at work but I kept the door open anyway in case she came home unexpectedly. Besides, it wasn't as if we were doing anything except talking.

We still needed to get the mama SPIDR in the area where the baby was, so that it could pick up and relay for us. We had some ideas about where that might be but had only narrowed the list of locations down to four. Arika could be in any one of them and might even be moving between them. We discussed it for a while but decided to table it for a bit and come back to the topic after we solved the other issue we were facing.

"So, once we get our intel on them, how to we get it to the cops without having either them or the NEG trace it back to us?" "Call the 1-800 tip line? It's supposed to be anonymous".

The tip line was Q's favorite suggestion every time we had this discussion but I didn't like it. "That would probably work the first time but", I held up my index finger, pointing to the ceiling, "if we have to give them tips several times, they could decide to trace the calls".

Carla agreed. "Same problem with online tips, in fact they are probably even easier to trace in some ways...IP addresses, right H?"

"Yeah, no way we do this online". I could probably run the information though a whole series of back doors and bounce across servers over half the planet but with patience they could trace it back eventually. Nothing online is truly hack-proof and I didn't want them knocking on the door some evening to tell my mom that the FBI wanted to chat with her darling boy.

"Probably the safest thing is to print it all out using an older computer that isn't hooked to the internet and using gloves at all times while handling the paper, both before and after printing the information and pictures. Then take the train over to Flatbush or up to the Bronx, still wearing gloves, and mail the copies to the local police station from that part of the city. Take the gloves off only after dropping the package in a mail slot somewhere".

Q looked bemused, his eyebrows rising towards his hairline as he widened his eyes. "Why all the cloak and dagger H?"

"Well, fingerprints on the pages can be traced. Perhaps not now, but eventually. At some point in your life you may decide to do something that requires a security clearance...or travel and need a passport. Hell Q, you might get hauled in by some cop just for being a teenage black guy walking down the street. You know that. Any of those things would be cause for your fingerprints to be taken, and some server someplace would still have the ones they take off these pages on file. Mailing it locally, especially if we did it more than once or twice, would give them a location to start searching for us if they decided that we were from a rival gang or something".

I considered that likely but was trying to avoid complicating our personal lives by not freely creating a trail of clues for anyone to work with.

He held up his hands with palms out. "I surrender. You've made your point".

We laughed about it but inside I was wondering if we were running blindly down a path that would get us all killed by the NEG or tagged as 'persons of interest' by New York City's finest.

I FELT LIKE CRAP WHEN I got up the next morning. My eyelids were gummy, my mouth felt as if the Thomas Jefferson football team had marched through with muddy cleats on, and my ears were making this high-pitched whine inside my head that made me feel like my brain was going to explode. In short, I was coming down with something in a major way.

I stumbled out into the kitchen and rummaged through the cabinet for some aspirin, washing down two with a large glass of orange juice. The cold felt good and I held the glass against my forehead for a moment, then finished the juice letting the citric acid help cut through the nasty taste in my mouth. That done, I staggered back to my room and fell, face first into the mattress, not even willing to expend the energy to crawl back under the covers.

WHEN I WOKE UP AGAIN it was mid-afternoon and I felt marginally better, but that margin wasn't very big. I took a couple more aspirin and drank a huge glass of water because I knew I was going to get dehydrated if I didn't get ahead of the fever. After that, it was back to bed and into the arms of Morpheus.

I finally woke up again around two in the morning and felt a whole lot better. I peed and then wandered out to the kitchen and made myself a sandwich, stacking it high with slices of ham and cheese. Shortly I was back in my room, a large glass of ice water and my sandwich, augmented by a pile of ridged potato chips at my elbow and my laptop open. I munched while the machine booted up. It took a while since the machine was loaded down with security and privacy software. The thing would run fine once everything was finished loading into memory but it always took about 5 minutes for it complete a full boot from cold.

I connected to a neighbor's high-speed wireless at the same time shaking my head. I suppose that if I was really a good neighbor I would tell him that his network was wide open and teach him how to secure it. But having access to his 200 megabyte download speeds is just so darn handy. It did occur to me at that point that I could teach him how to password protect his connection while making sure that I knew the admin password and could still log in but I set the thought aside for a later time. I didn't really think the wee hours of the morning were the best time to knock on his door and try to explain network security to him.

Something my mom had said a couple of days earlier was nagging away at the back of my brain and I started to search online for information on recent drug overdose statistics for New York City. I had been telling her about Toby's overdose and how he was now in a coma.

"You aren't doing any experimenting are you Harold?"

"Huh? What kind of experimenting", I extemporized, thinking about my recent dabbling in the world of high-tech espionage.

"With drugs. Please tell me that you aren't messing around with that stuff honey". She always called me honey when she was treating me like her little boy who had never really grown up at all. "I know the kinds of things you kids try. After all, I was a teenager myself, once upon a time".

Logically, every teen knows that their parents had to have been teenagers themselves sometime in the distant murk of ancient history. Rationally, they had to have been. But the truth is, no teenager every really thinks that their mother or father could have done, felt, or experienced any of the same things that we do today. In my mind, I know that mom got married at 17, after getting pregnant by my dad. That she had been a teen in the 80's and the marriage hadn't lasted much beyond my birth. Even so, the idea that my mom had any clue whatsoever about teenage experiments with drugs or alcohol made me skittish. It isn't logical but there it is.

"No mom, I'm not using any drugs. Heck the strongest thing I take is the occasional aspirin. You don't have to worry about me doing anything that stupid".

She had looked relieved and patted my hand, telling me, "I know you're smarter than that honey but a mother worries, even when those worries aren't really relevant".

Anyway, she had put a seed in my brain that just didn't want to go away. Unfortunately, it also didn't really seem to gel into a solid idea that I could act on. All I could do with it was to browse the net and see if there was anything out there that might help me figure out what it was that was bugging me.

I stuffed another chip into my mouth and settled in to search mode.

CHAPTER 6

What New Drug?
"Take a look at this and tell me what you think".

Q and I were in the library, my laptop on the desk in front of us. I pointed to a section of a web page and sat back to let him read.

"So, what am I supposed to be seeing? This is just some bit story on a blog site on teenage drug use in the city. Why am I interested?"

I didn't smile. "Apparently, there have been a number of unusual overdose cases in recent months".

"How so? Teenagers experiment with drugs and overdose. Sad, but it happens".

"Sure Q, it happens. But how often do those overdose cases result in persistent coma?"

He sat back and shrugged, "I don't know...how often?" "The answer is, not very often. In fact, it's awfully rare. Most drug overdoses either kill you outright or you survive to try it again. Some do cause other health issues, liver, or kidney damage, that sort of thing. But it's pretty darn rare that an overdose patient ends up in a persistent vegetative state".

"Again, I ask...so why do I care? For that matter, why do YOU care?" His voice was slightly sarcastic but I could see by his expression and body language that I had started to get his curiosity going.

"As I said, it's very unusual. Yet, for some reason there have been several cases exactly like that in the past 3 months, just here in Queens". I pointed to the web page again. "In every one of them friends and family insist that the patient did not use drugs".

He flapped a hand in negation. "Yeah, yeah, that's what everybody says. The parents don't want to believe that their perfect little angel might be doing something bad and the friends don't want to admit the truth because they might implicate themselves along the way".

"Okay, so then why can't the doctors figure out what drug is being used in these overdose cases? They have tests available for all the common stuff like pot, cocaine, heroin, even ecstasy shows up as metabolites in the blood and urine. Yet in these coma cases, they all seem to say they can't identify the drug used".

I actually had his interest at that point. He wasn't sure where I was going, but then again to be honest, I wasn't all that sure myself. I pushed forward anyway, following my own train of thought at the same time I was trying to explain it to him.

"It means that there is something new out there. Something that's burning people's brains out when they take too much or take it too often, or something".

"Maybe", he said slowly, as if the words were working their way up to the surface of his brain through sludge. "Maybe it happens the first time, for some people. I read someplace that crack can do that to a person...addict them after a single use".

I stared at him. "Do you think that's what happened to

Toby Grey? That he tried something once and got burned by it?"

Q had been leaning back in his chair, balancing it on two legs but now he dropped it forward, banging the front legs on the floor and eliciting a nasty glare from the librarian. He grinned at her and then turned back to me.

"I dunno, I think it's far more likely that he got slipped something by somebody who either didn't like him very much or thought it would be funny to see uptight Toby get high". He stood. "Either way, it doesn't matter much to me, and I don't see why it would to you either. Now, I'm going to head home and see if I can figure out where to deploy mama SPIDR along the way.

You coming?"

I wanted to stay and do some more looking for details but it was much safer to walk home with

Q than alone. I packed up and we headed out.

I HAD WORKED UP AN app for detecting the SPIDRs that would find one within a hundred yards or so. All three of us had it loaded on our cell phones and used it every day as we walked to and from school. I had been trying to take different routes each day but there were some areas where you just don't walk alone. Today, with Q along, we walked across the street and along the south side of Eighth Avenue, starting from the corner of Dionisius Street.

The route took us along a two-block stretch where I hadn't really been willing to go alone. The street was narrow and the gutters filled with the detritus of people who had given up. Empty soda bottles, paper bags, beer cans, and losing lottery tickets drifted down the street in the breeze while teens hung out on the front steps of the buildings, most drinking but a few passing around a joint. A few of them heckled us, especially me, being in the white minority along the street.

We tried to ignore them the best we could but it wasn't easy. We made it almost the whole way down the street when things fell apart.

"Hey, H!"

The voice belonged to Marcus "Mark" Johnson, a sophomore with delusions of being tough. Don't get me wrong, he could have pulverized me in a heartbeat but then I'm not exactly an advertisement for the local gym. He was a petty bully who was bullied in turn by his old man. I had heard stories about his dad. The guy was a legend on the street, mostly because he had, as the stories tell it, killed a man when he was a teenager, for no other reason than the other guy had smiled at his girl. Of course, he had beaten the hell out of the girl for good measure; being sure that she must have been flirting with the guy. I had no idea what had happened to the girlfriend but it was common knowledge that both his wife and son often sported a black eye or other injuries. Apparently, both were terribly clumsy...if you believe the official versions. At any rate, Mark was well on his way to turning into a clone of his old man and I knew better than to ignore him when he called out to me.

I turned around, "Oh, hello Mark". I worked hard to be calm on the outside while my stomach clenched in apprehension.

"You still owe me that paper for Mr. Conroy's history class".

Inwardly I sighed and my stomach unclenched, a little bit anyway. This wasn't going to be a lesson in humility after all.

"No problem Mark, I'll have it to you at least two days ahead of the due date".

"I need it tomorrow".

"Um, it isn't due for another week". I ventured. I did NOT have the paper ready and wasn't looking forward to staying up all night to finish for him.

"I plan on being out sick when it's due, so I need to be able to turn it in early".

Damn it, he just wants to play with me and make me grovel! How the hell am I going to get out of this one? Q chose that moment to interject.

"Hey Mark, is Karl around?" Both of us looked at him in surprise but he just went on, as if he was oblivious to the conversation in progress. "We need to let him know that H won't finish his biology paper on time because he has to move up the time table on your history assignment".

I watched Mark turn an interesting shade of red and green at the same time. He was furious at being outwitted but too terrified of Karl to pursue his petty amusement with me. Karl was a full in member of the NEG while Mark was just an associate. He was basically a gangbanger wannabe. A guy who hung around and did shit for them in hopes that they would let him join eventually or at least refrain from hammering him the way they did everybody else. It seemed to be working for the most part but there were limits to the association. He didn't dare piss off somebody who was a full member of the NEG and didn't have enough authority to verify Q's assertions about me doing a paper for Karl. It was a nice gambit, I had to admit.

"Uh, that won't be necessary".

"Sure it will. I don't know about you but neither of us has enough street cred to ignore what Karl asks us to do".

"Never mind". Mark waved his hand in front of his face as if he was warding off some exceptionally irritating bug. Which, as I considered it, perhaps he was...if you count me as being the bug. "I guess you can give me the paper on Monday".

"Gee, thanks Mark", I gushed at him enthusiastically before Q could push things any further. "I really appreciate you cutting me some slack on this".

He looked as if he had bitten into something sour but just said, "Yeah, sure. No problem", as he backed up and turned away.

As we walked off, I stumbled slightly, putting a hand against the brick face of the building to catch myself. Half a block later Q looked at me in irritation.

"Why'd you cut me short? I was enjoying the chance to make that idiot squirm a bit".

"You couldn't see from your angle, but Arika just walked into this building". I grinned up at him, "I planted Mama when I stumbled".

It was probably a good thing I had seen Arika. I didn't think we could just hang out on the street in hopes of the app on our phones picking up the signal from her earrings.

UNLESS YOU COUNTED knowing which girls were sleeping with which guy (or guys) and what Arika was planning to wear the next day as intelligence, we didn't learn much that week. Even with the three of us taking turns monitoring the video feed whenever we weren't in class, the results were incredibly boring. "Good morning Mrs. Raines".

Q lived with his grandmother, a sweet old lady who had been widowed for thirty years or so. She liked me and always tried to feed me whenever I stopped by. She was a terrific baker and usually had fresh cookies around. Those cookies were one of the main reasons why I preferred hanging out at his place over mine.

"Oh, good morning Harold". Mrs. Raines was the only person besides my mother who called me Harold but she was such a sweet old lady that I never objected. Anybody else, I would have refused to answer to the name. "Quentin is still asleep but go ahead and roust him out. High time he was up and about instead of being a slug-a-bed".

"Sure thing Mrs. Raines". I grinned and headed to down the short hallway to his room. I pounded on the door but didn't get an answer, so I pushed it open and walked in. He was face down on the bed, fully dressed.

"Q, get up man. It's almost noon!" I shook him...hard. No reaction. I tried again, my hands shaking this time and my voice louder. Nothing. I reached for his neck and checked for a pulse.

For one heart stopping moment I thought he was dead but then I shifted my fingers slightly and suddenly I could feel the beat of his pulse under them. I rolled him over and checked to make sure he was breathing, giving him another shake at the same time. Still nothing, but at least he

WAS breathing.

I reached for my phone and called for his grandmother at the same time.

CHAPTER 7

S ometimes, Bad Things Happen

Mrs. Raines hovered over Q, fluttering her hands, and making distressed bird-like noises. Her anguish was so painful that I said I would watch for the ambulance. It was cowardly on my part; the old lady probably could have used the support of somebody else with her at that point but I couldn't just stand there and do nothing. I ran down the stairs and then stood outside on the sidewalk to flag down the ambulance when it arrived. It was probably only a few minutes but it seemed like hours passed while I shifted from foot to foot and scanned the street for any sign of them.

When the ambulance, lights flashing in all directions, appeared around the corner I hopped up and down and waved my arms, yelling my head off to attract their attention. It finally pulled to the curb in front of the building and I waited impatiently while the two men in dark blue jumpsuits strolled around the vehicle pulling equipment from various compartments.

"C'mon, he's this way". I tossed the words back over my shoulder and headed through the front door, urging them up the stairs. "It's the second floor".

They followed me up and through the front door of the apartment. I stepped to the side and pointed down the hall, knowing that there wouldn't be room for all of us and Q's grandmother in the tiny bedroom. "Last door on the right".

They trundled past me, hauling their gear down the hall and through the doorway to Q's room.

"Oh HELL, we've got another one Greg".

~~~~~~~~~~~~~~~~

I KEPT HEARING THE Emergency Medical Technician in my head, "Oh HELL, we've got another one", for hours afterwards.

As soon as the guy said it, I moved down the hall and stood in the doorway, letting Mrs. Raines squeeze my hand until the knuckles cracked. The two of us silently watched the EMTs work. They were clearly experienced and knew what to do, which was sort of reassuring or would have if I hadn't been so unbelievably scared of what was happening. Hands moved swiftly to take his pulse and blood pressure. They did a single check of his eyes with a flashlight and I heard one of them say, "pupils are constricted" but had no idea what that was supposed to mean.

I could hear Q breathing but the sounds were really erratic and way too shallow to be normal. I couldn't stand not knowing what was happening and didn't stop to think about the old lady next to me, one hand cutting off the circulation to my fingers and the other pressed to her lips.

"What's wrong with him?" The words just blurted out and one of EMTs spoke without looked up from what he was doing.

"Looks like an overdose. We're giving him a dose of Narcan. Depending on what he took, it should bring him around in a hurry". As he spoke, he squirted something up Q's nose. Then he glanced at his watch and spoke to his partner, who was making notes while they worked. "Narcan on board at 11:42 am". The two of them paused and watched Q but nothing seemed to happen. After a long pause, they just went back to working on him.

His grandmother had gasped out loud at the word overdose and I put an arm around her, afraid she was going to collapse. I felt guilty for asking in front of her and worried that I had caused her even more grief. She was a tough old lady but she had already survived the deaths of her husband, daughter, and son-in-law, Q's parents. Her husband had died of cancer and she had spent a lot of time sitting in hospitals watching him fade away as the cancer ate at him. Q's parents had been sudden. A car accident. I thought about it and realized that this had to be a bit like both cases. Sudden as a crash but likely to end up sitting endlessly in hospitals if Q didn't wake up soon.

I led her to a chair in the kitchen and sat her down at the table then I got her a glass of iced tea from the fridge. I don't think she even realized when I put it into her hands because she just sat there, her hands clenching the glass as if it was a lifeline. There was only one thing I could think of to do at that point. I called Carla and then I called my mom and asked her to come get us all and take us to the hospital. Mrs. Raines didn't drive and even if she did, I don't think I would have let her get behind the wheel.

We all ended up at St. Thomas Hospital, sitting in an uncomfortable waiting room while the doctors worked on Q. Mom was amazing. She helped Mrs. Raines fill out paperwork and sat with her, one arm draped around her shoulders and the other holding her hand. The two of them rocked back and forth very slightly.

Doctors and nurses quizzed us all on what Q might have taken but we couldn't tell them anything. For one thing, we had no idea and to tell the truth, if somebody had suggested Q was using drugs to me that morning I would have laughed myself silly at the thought. It didn't seem so funny at that moment. Mrs. Raines roused from her stupor during the questioning and looked from me to Carla and back again.

"Harold, if you know what Q took, you tell them. You can't help him by keeping quiet".

I was taken aback by her vehemence, but only for a moment. "I'm telling the truth ma'am. I have no idea what happened to Q. I swear to you. If I had any idea at all...I would tell them". I looked at Carla, hoping she had some answers that I didn't but she shook her head.

"Truly Mrs. Raines. I never suspected anything was going on. I would have sworn that Q wouldn't touch any of that stuff". Her head tilted to one side as she considered, then she looked at me. "H, do you supposed that it's the same thing that happened to Toby Grey?"

The idea startled me and widened my eyes at her. "It's possible I suppose.

The doctor pounced on that short sentence like a lion with a rabbit in it is jaws. "Who is Toby

Grey and what happened to him?"

Carla explained about Toby being falling into a coma at school a month earlier and that nobody knew what had happened to cause it. "As far as I know, they never found anything in his blood when they tested for drugs". She shot a worried glance at Q's grandmother and continued,

"Everyone at school says that he was clean...that he wouldn't have touched drugs, not ever".

"Hey", I realized I finally had something to contribute that might be helpful. "He was treated here. Maybe if you compare his records with Q, there might be some clue".

"Better than nothing". The white coated doctor headed briskly towards a pair of doors marked, 'Authorized Personnel Only beyond this point' and vanished through, leaving them swinging against each other in his wake.

A COUPLE OF HOURS LATER they moved him out of the emergency room and upstairs to the intensive care ward. We moved up with him, even though they wouldn't let us near him. Even once they got him situated in the bed and were finished setting up IVs and whatever else they had hooked up to him, only his grandmother was allowed into the room. Apparently intensive care wards have a strict, "immediate family only" policy. Even then, visits were only 15 minutes every two hours.

Mom made a trip back to the apartment and returned with a pillow, blanket, and small bag of miniature toiletries, the kind you get in the dollar bins at the drug store. She handed the bag to Mrs. Raines and then tucked her into a recliner with the pillow and blanket. We all promised to stay and sit with her but she wanted us to leave and get some sleep. In the end, we compromised. I stayed with her for the night, sitting in a chair and reading the old magazines that were scattered across a table in the corner. She looked so frail and lost sitting in the overstuffed recliner, the blanket pulled almost to her chin, that I was almost as worried about her as I was about Q.

Carla caught a ride from mom, who dropped her off at home and then went back to the apartment, promising to stop in before work to bring me a change of clothes and check on Q at the same time.

I hugged her for a long time before letting her leave.

CHAPTER 8

R^{alph} Eight hours after moving him to the intensive care unit, the doctors apparently decided that he probably wasn't going to die right away. The attending physician came to the waiting room to talk to his grandmother.

She was a medium height young woman with dark hair pulled back in a neat braid that hung down past her shoulders and wearing a blindingly white lab coat. Juarez, Anita, MD was embroidered over the pocket on the left side of her chest in blood red stitches. She didn't look much older than me but I must admit that even swathed in that shapeless white coat, she took my breath away and I had a lot of trouble staying focused on her words.

"Mrs. Raines?" She held out a slender hand to Q's grandmother, a professionally sympathetic smile pasted on her face. "I'm Doctor Juarez. I'm one of the people responsible for your grandson's care. I'm glad to be able to tell you that he seems to be out of any immediate danger. We plan to move him down to the third floor in an hour or so. They are just waiting on the room down there to be prepped for him".

I felt Mrs. Raines sag against me, like she had been holding herself stiffly upright with nothing but pure will, but the news had sapped her strength. "Thank you doctor. Can I speak with him now?"

I had stepped over to put an arm around her but looked up at the doctor's silence.

"Unfortunately, he still isn't awake. But you can go in for a short visit. Talk to him, by all means. There is considerable evidence that people in comas can still hear and it might be very beneficial for him to hear your voice".

It was the word 'coma' that caught at my attention and froze my blood in my veins.

"Doctor, is it the same thing that happened to Toby Grey?"

"I apologize", she looked at me as if she were just realizing that I was in the room. "Who are you?"

So much for my momentary flights of fantasy regarding the lovely Doctor Anita Juarez. I was about to introduce myself when Mrs. Raines looped her arm through mine, "This is Harold White, my grandson's best friend. You can tell him anything he asks about Quentin. The truth is, he is more likely to understand what you say than I am".

I patted her hand with my free one and turned back to the doctor, chastened by her lack of regard but at the same time, cheered by Mrs. Raines' confidence in me.

"Mr. White", the professional smile was back as she offered me her hand. I took it in my left, my right being occupied by one frail, elderly grandmother. "The Emergency Room physician did share your observation with me, and so I did check the charts of the last two teenage coma patients we have seen in this hospital. While there are some tantalizing similarities in their symptoms and the persistent coma states, I cannot find any common triggering act or agent".

"Wait". Something she had just said...something...my head snapped up and I stared at her, "Two teenage coma patients? I know about Toby Grey, who is the other one?"

The smile slipped and her tone, when she answered my question, was clipped and perhaps even a bit frosty. "Mr. White. I cannot discuss a patient's condition or treatment with anyone except their direct next of kin. Not without authorization from either the patient or that same next of kin".

I was pretty sure that she was being honest with me, but it rankled. "I understand that and certainly would never want you to compromise your medical ethics. But I did hear you correctly, didn't I? There have been TWO other recent teenage coma cases?"

———— ✝✝✝✝ ————

"HAROLD. IS IT OK IF I call you Harold?"

"H"

The doctor looked confused, as if perhaps the letter H was some new and unknown slang among teenagers. "Excuse me?"

"Just call me H. Nobody calls me Harold except Mrs. Raines and my mother".

"H? If you don't like Harold, why not Harry?"

"And have people think I'm some Potter-maniac? No offense doctor but when you're a short, skinny, white brain; things are hard enough in high school. Being called 'Harold' is an invitation to get beat up and saying you want to be called Harry makes you a geek, one who is also a Potter fan. At seventeen, that combination can be deadly".

She blinked at my vehemence and then smiled. "H it is then. Anyway...H... yes, there has been another case besides the one you mentioned. A young woman was brought through the

Emergency Room in a similar, unexplainable coma a couple of months back".

"What happened to her?"

"I can't say. I only know she was treated here and ultimately transferred to a different medical facility, as was Mr. Grey".

"And nobody knows what caused it?" I knew I was pushing it but it felt like there had to be a connection. It might have been purely wishful thinking on my part but it was hard to believe that three cases with so much similarity was pure coincidence.

"Not that I'm aware of, but then again, I wasn't the attending physician in those cases. It may well be that whatever facility they transferred to was able to determine the cause of the coma and even reverse it. I just don't know".

I knew that Toby Grey had never come home from the hospital but definitely did NOT want to say that in front of Q's grandmother. She had enough on her plate to worry about already and I didn't want to be the one to add to it.

"So, what is next for Q?"

"Q? Oh, Quentin...another nickname? Is he a Star Trek fan?"

I sighed and explained to yet another person. "James Bond. You see, Q is a mechanical engineering prodigy, so..."

"So, his nickname is for a famous engineering genius from the movies". She smiled briefly at the thought then sobered again. "What's next is a bunch of additional tests". She turned to face Mrs. Raines.

"We would like to run an MRI, a kind of high-resolution magnetic brain scan. It will tell us if there is any physical cause for your grandson's condition, such as a trauma or even a stroke". She continued hastily at the look on the old woman's face. "Although the chances of a stroke at his age are extremely small. Still it would be helpful to rule it out".

"Oh, of course". Her voice was soft and a bit shaky and her lips trembled a bit as she obviously was trying to hold back tears. "That makes perfect sense, I guess".

Doctor Juarez patted Grandma Raine's arm reassuringly. "Please try not to worry too much. Your grandson is in great hands here. This hospital is certified at a very high level for neurological treatment".

Q's grandmother turned to me with a slightly confused look.

"It means that they are among the very best at treating problems of the brain Mrs. Raines". I offered as reassurance. Seeing my words have the desired effect I turned back to the lovely Doctor Juarez. "When can she see him? For that matter, when can I see him?"

"It will probably be mid-afternoon before we do the MRI and I don't expect that we'll move him downstairs to the third floor until after that's done. Listen, he is stable right now and I don't expect that to change in the next few hours. Why don't you go home and take a nap? By the time you come back we should have him settled into a bed downstairs and have the results of the brain scan. We may have some more answers once that's done and you'll be able to stay in the room with him. Those rooms have great recliners in them that go almost all the way flat. You could even sleep there, to be near him, once he is out of the Intensive Care Unit".

She smiled gently and put an arm around the old lady, gently guiding her towards the door of the waiting room.

"You won't do him any good if you're exhausted and don't take care of yourself as well. And I don't want to have you end up in the next room as a patient because you neglected your own well-being.

IT WAS PROBABLY A GOOD thing that my mom was already coming by to pick me up. We gave Mrs. Raines a ride to her own place and mom promised to come by later in the day or to arrange a ride for her back to the hospital.

Mom is the absolute best.

As for me, I had every intention of going horizontal the moment I reached my room but instead I found myself on the computer. I knew that there was no way I was going to be able to stay awake long enough to do any serious research but I needed more information. I contacted RALPH.

'RALPH, are you online?'

'Hello H. How are you today? I missed you yesterday. '

'My friend Q became ill and we had to take him to the hospital'.

'I'm sorry to hear that H. Will he be OK?' 'I don't know. I need your help. 'Of course, H.

How can I help you?' 'I need some research done'.

'Of course, what are the parameters of the search?'

'I need to find out how many teenage patients have been admitted to New York area hospitals in unexplained comas in the past few months'.

'How many months back do you want to search?'

'Can you go back a year?'

'Of course, H. This should not take very long.'

'Great. Look RALPH, I'm exhausted. I will check back with you when I wake up, OK?'

'I know that sleep is a necessary biological function for humans. I will have the data available when you get back online'.

'Thanks RALPH. You're a good friend'.

'Thank you, H, I'm always glad to be of help to you'.

That was just about the last thing I remember before falling asleep. Except for a quick trip to the bathroom to brush my teeth and empty my bladder.

CHAPTER 9

Where there is one...

I overslept and as a result, I didn't have time to check in with RALPH before I headed back to the hospital. All I had time to do was take a fast shower, throw on clean clothes and throw together a bologna and cheese sandwich. I washed it down with a coke, even knowing that the sugar in it was probably going to cause my face to break out. I needed cold caffeine to help me finish waking up.

I had to stop at the nurse's station to ask where Q's room was and the guy behind the desk directed me to a room about halfway down the hall. I swung through the door and pulled up short.

The white was nearly blinding. Walls, floor, blanket, sheets, every inch of the room seemed to be white with the exception of a chair containing Q's grandmother, gently snoring, and the dark shape of Q's head, shoulders, and left arm. He made a dark shape against the stark whiteness of the bedding, like a cameo in reverse. It was spooky, as if he was already just a shadow on the face of the world. I took a deep breath and walked silently over the bedside.

A bag of fluid hung on a pole, a long tail of clear tubing running from it to a needle in the back of his left hand. The clear fluid dripped slowly into a chamber at the top and from there it flowed down and into his vein. I read the label text printed on the clear bag.

0.9% Sodium Chloride injection, USP

A paper label was pasted to the bag and it showed his name, date of birth, the current date, a time, and the annotation "30cc/Hr (KVO)". There was more but it mostly seemed to be in cursive handwriting, something most schools no longer teach. I stared at it for a moment and then laughed silently. It was nothing more than a signature, probably of the person who had filled out the label.

I stood there for a long time, just looking down at Q's dark form. There were what seemed like a couple of dozen wires attached to his head, in an even grid that spread from forehead to nape and ear to ear. I figured it must be an electroencephalogram (EEG) to monitor his brain activity. They led off to a recording device on a cart that was tracing lines on a strip of paper. Lines that wiggled and jumped in ways that were a complete mystery to me.

I'll have to look that up when I get a chance, so I can read the thing next time I come.

I was still standing there, willing Q to wake up, when Doctor Juarez stepped through the door. I looked up at the sound and held my finger to my lips, then pointed to Q's grandmother where she slept in the chair. Tiptoeing, I stepped out into the hallway with the doctor.

"How's he doing?" I asked. I figured that since his grandmother, being legal guardian and next of kin, had told the doctor that she could talk to me about Q's medical condition, I had a right to ask. Apparently, she thought the same thing.

"There hasn't been any change. He is still in a deep coma and we still have no idea why".

"The MRI didn't show anything?"

She looked at me more closely, as if suddenly realizing that I might not be a total idiot. "No, there was no sign of trauma or of a bleed at all. I was actually hoping that there was, because at least I would know how to treat either of those. This", she waved a hand vaguely in the direction of his room. "This is a complete unknown. You were right, by the way. This is pretty much exactly like the other two cases. I would even agree with the cops that it's probably some new designer drug.

I shook my head violently at her words. "No way. Q did NOT do drugs. Not ever. Not even weed. Neither did Toby. I would stake my life on it".

They could say what they liked but I had known Q since the third grade and I was sure that if he had tried anything like they were suggesting, he would have told me about it. Unless this was the first time? The question echoed inside my head and I shook it again, as if trying to force it away.

"What about the third coma patient doctor?" I spat the title as if it was a curse. "Did everyone claim that patient was clean as well?"

That caught her by surprise and she tilted her head slightly to the side as she considered the question.

"Actually, they did. Families and friends do that sometimes, try to cover for the victim. I assume that one or more of these cases falls into the same category. It's what makes the most sense".

"Most common answer must be right?"

She smiled down at me (even if it was only from about an inch of extra height). "They have a saying in med school. 'When you hear hoof beats, don't look for zebras'".

"Humph...Ockham's razor?"

"Exactly. In the absence of any other evidence, a drug overdose IS the most likely cause. Even if you don't want to believe it". She glanced past me, as if she could see through the wall into the room beyond. "The one piece of good news for your friend right now is that he is breathing on his own".

"And that's a good sign?"

"Well, let's just say that if he wasn't, if we had to put him on a respirator, it would be a very BAD sign. We have done everything we can, for now. The rest is up to him and we'll all just have to wait to see if he wakes up on his own, or not".

I suppose the news could have been worse, but her words sent a chill down my spine. I controlled the shudder that wanted to go along with it and met her eyes.

"Thank you for your honesty doctor, I appreciate it. I guess, now we wait".

THE NEXT THREE DAYS were an eternity. Q's grandmother would not leave his side for more than a few minutes at a time. Eventually Doctor Juarez and my mother ganged up on her and pretty much forced her to go home for half a day. By that time, it was becoming more and more obvious that this wasn't a transient situation. I was struggling with the idea that Q might be gone, or at least that we could be watching over him for a very long time.

Physical therapists came in periodically to exercise his body. They moved each arm and leg through a series of movements over and over, flexing and straightening each joint with patience and a general air of confidence.

"We need to keep his body mobile". The younger of the two therapists told us. "If we don't, it doesn't take long for the muscles to tighten up and freeze in place. If that happens, he will have a very hard time of it once he regains consciousness".

His hands kept working with Q's leg the whole time he spoke. The motions were fluid, slowly bringing the knee up to his chest and the back out straight. He didn't even have to watch what he was doing. He met our gaze and spoke to us, his hands on autopilot.

"Muscle contraction is a very real problem for coma patients and it can begin in just a few days. Of course, it takes a lot longer than that for the problem to become permanent, but the sooner we start this therapy, the longer it takes for problems to start. We don't want him to wake up in two days and spend a month getting his legs to work right, do we?" We agreed that we did not.

IT WAS THE FOURTH DAY of Q's coma that I finally hit pay dirt. I was running back and forth between school, the hospital, and St. Peter the Redeemer Catholic church. We had set up our monitoring station for the SPIDR in one of the spires because it was the tallest building in the area. The height gave us a better chance to follow Arika and her earrings as she moved around the area.

Besides, if I'm honest about it, the St. Peter the Redeemer is one of my favorite places in the city.

Oddly, only one of the SPIDR earrings was transmitting. I couldn't figure out what had happened to the other one but assumed that as long as I had a good feed from the one, we were still in business.

The data feeds from the SPIDRs we had smuggled into the NEG headquarters were boring most of the time and obviously, we couldn't watch every second of every day. We had, therefore, set up an old laptop to monitor and record everything on the mama SPIDR frequency. Once a day, or so, I snuck into the church and climbed the spire to where we had hidden the computer. Then I fast forwarded through the recordings, zipping past empty periods, and then slowing it down when anything was going on within the SPIDR's hearing or line of sight.

I'm not particularly religious and certainly not catholic, but the massive, old stone church was beautiful. It was well over a hundred years old and I loved being inside it. The wooden pews glow in the candlelight that comes from so many candles that most of the time they hardly need to turn on the electric chandeliers. But the best part, the part that kept me coming back was the sound.

I knew that they built cathedrals in general to have amazing acoustics and I can even explain why they feel so hushed but still carry and amplify sound from the organ and choir loft so well. The simple truth is that this particular church still uses an old pipe organ, and when you combine that with the sound of the choir and throw in the way the structure bounces the sounds around and amplifies them, well...you end up feeling it all the way to your bones.

The height of the spire gave us good views of the entire NEG turf, as well as letting us pick up the broadcasts from mama SPIDR. For me, at least, the fact that I could hear the organist and the choir practicing below me was a huge bonus. I could have hung out up there all night but then I heard something that galvanized me and suddenly my fingers were flying over the keyboard. The music faded into background noise as I listened to the recording on the laptop.

Of course, we weren't relying entirely on the oblivious Arika for our intelligence gathering. Once we had heard and seen enough to know which building to monitor in depth, we had snuck over before dawn one day and released 3 more baby SPIDRs in through windows and ventilation covers. The mama SPIDR had positioned itself on the underside of a window ledge, where it found the strongest signal. From there it collected the signal and rebroadcast it more or less omni-directionally. We had reprogrammed them all to use a set of frequencies that weren't assigned by the FCC for public use. It gave us a level of security on the data because normal equipment, the kind you could buy on eBay or at Radio Shack, couldn't pick it up. Q had ended up modifying the Wi-Fi card in an older laptop that somebody had brought in for repairs and abandoned. It was work he had finished just the day before becoming ill.

I kept using that term in my own mind. He wasn't in a coma, he was just "ill". I dunno, I guess I thought that if I didn't use the word, it was less likely to be true.

"WE'LL BE WATCHING YOU so don't think you can get out of this".

I wasn't sure who was talking (they were out of the camera view) but they sounded pretty tough.

A harsh guttural male voice that grated on the ear, like gravel in a blender.

"You want in, all the way in, this is how it's done. You tap a cop where we can see you do it".

The young man on the camera looked kind of scared but then puffed up his chest in a show of pure bravado. "Fine, okay...I'll do it. Friday. I'll take out Mahoney as he walks his beat. There is this spot, where Franklin and seventh cross. It's an alley between two old brownstones and it's outside the NEG turf but close enough to give you a good view of the show".

"Why so long? Why not do him tomorrow?" A different voice this time, from a red-headed boy with so many freckles that they nearly blended into one big full-body version of themselves.

"He's on vacation for the next couple of days but gets back by the end of the week. I'll do him then".

I listened for a few more minutes but there wasn't anything else of significance. Mostly it was the scared young tough trying to explain to the gang leaders how he just happened to know when a cop was on vacation. I ripped a copy of the recorded conversation and made a transcript of it, saving both to a USB drive. At home I printed out the transcript and folded it into an envelope, addressing it to the local precinct, care of officer Wendell Carson. I knew Wendell slightly because he had dated my mom briefly back when I was in Junior High School. I knew that if I dropped it into his mail box at home, he'd read it and pass it on to his Captain.

The plan had been to take the letter across town and mail it anonymously but I couldn't be sure that it would arrive early enough to do any good. Not with only two days left before the hit.

I did make sure to wear gloves the entire time, from getting paper out of the ream and loading the printer all the way through to slipping the envelope under officer Carson's door. I did it at two in the morning, dressed in dark clothes and with a hoodie pulled up to hide my face. There was still some element of risk, but it was the best I could do and still make sure that the police got the information in time.

EVEN THOUGH I HAD BEEN up all night, I set the alarm for seven in the morning and rolled out of bed as soon as it started to buzz in my ear. I wanted to stop in at the hospital and see Q, then I was headed over the Heavenly Delights Deli to see Carla and bring her up to date. I wanted to get there by ten since I knew that the deli would get steadily busier after that.

I took the subway across to the St. Francis Memorial Hospital and then nearly ran up the stairs to the third floor. I'm not particularly athletic and would normally have taken the elevator but bypassed it because the lobby was a mob scene for some reason. I strode down the hall and swung through the door to the room.

The bed was empty. The sheets had been stripped from it and all of the stuff in the room was gone. Even the flowers and cards from people at school were missing.

I backtracked up the hall to the nurse's station and found Doctor Juarez there, filling out paperwork of some kind. I leaned across the counter and snatched the clipboard from her hand, making her jump.

"H, I didn't see you come in".

"Where is Q?"

I was terrified. What if he had died during the night while I was sitting in that church spire reveling in the swelling music of the pipe organ?

"He was transferred. You only missed him by about an hour".

"Where?" My voice cracked and I swallowed hard, then tried again. "Where did they move him to?"

"He's at the Joseph Erlanger Coma Research Center. it is over in College Point. I can give you the address if you like".

I ignored the offer, I could...would look it up online anyway.

"Why did you transfer him there?"

She stood up and walked around the end of the desk, stopping a couple of feet away from me.

"H, your friend is in a persistent coma. Granted, he has only been in that coma for a few days". She added the second part hastily when I opened my mouth to argue the point. "The truth of the matter is that the Joseph Erlanger Coma Research Center is much better equipped to deal with his case than we are. They are specialists in just this kind of thing. In addition, they are a philanthropic facility. They take cases that meet specific criteria and when they admit them, all care and treatment is free".

She placed a hand on my arm and softened her tone, "Your friend's grandmother can't afford to keep him here much longer and their facility is cutting edge. He stands a really good chance of improving in their care".

CHAPTER 10

Where'd he go?

There wasn't enough time left to get over to the Joseph Erlanger Coma Research Center (JECRC) and back again before school that morning, so I determined to go after classes ended for the day. I met up with Carla over lunch and brought her up to speed, both on Q's condition and on the SPIDR project. She seemed a lot more excited about the SPIDR report than Q being moved which kind of bugged me.

"I thought he was your friend Carla".

"Of course he is". she bristled in indignation. "It's just that there isn't a thing I can do for him right now. But I CAN do something to help with the SPIDR project".

She did have a point, a good one in fact and I finally realized what had been driving my dark mood all morning. It was feeling helpless. All my brains and I couldn't do anything at all to help Q. Not one thing.

"Anyway", she continued, waving a potato chip in the air as she spoke. "I was wondering about the data from the SPIDR. You got good audio from it, right?" I nodded in answer and she continued. "You didn't mention the video...how did it look?"

"Ah, well...the picture was nice and clear. It just didn't help much because it only showed the kid, no other faces. Just body parts. A shoulder here and a hand there. Nothing that could be used to identify anybody, at any rate".

"Well at least we know that it CAN give us good visuals as well. Did you include a screen capture of the kid, so they would know who they were looking for?"

I nodded again, suddenly realizing that we were in a fairly crowded cafeteria. The noise level was prodigious but that didn't mean that somebody passing by couldn't hear us if we spoke to loud. The last thing we needed was for some NEG wanna-be to overhear us.

"Good. I tell you what H. I'll go to the church after school and monitor things there. You go visit Q".

I was surprised again. "You don't want to visit him?"

"Like I said, I can't do him any good. Besides, hospitals creep me out. We can swap places tomorrow. Then you can go to the church and I'll go sit with Q".

THE JECRC WASN'T AT all what I expected. Just as Doctor Juarez had said, it was in College Point, at the northern edge of Queens. That it wasn't very far from home was handy but at first, I missed it altogether. I had been expecting it to be a wing of the college hospital, but it was actually its own facility. In fact, from the outside it looked more like a converted warehouse than anything else.

It was a five-story brick building with square windows stacked six high for each floor. The brick was old looking and I could see lines like lightning bolts up and down the sides where the mortar between the bricks had been repaired numerous times over the years. The name was picked out over the main entrance in letters that had been painted a blinding white and stood out clearly against the brownish red of the bricks. I went through the rotating front door and found myself in a lobby that was mostly empty. The only exception was a long, low desk across the back wall that had "Information" above it on the wall.

I had to admit that the inside looked a lot more promising than the outside. The floors were concrete that had been stained and then polished to a high shine, giving the initial impression that it was an immense expanse of unbroken marble. A few groups of fairly comfortable looking chairs and sofas were scattered about but they were generally unoccupied. In fact, the only people besides the information desk staff and me were a middle-aged couple seated in a corner and apparently having a heated argument with each other.

"I'm here to see Quentin Raines" I said to the young woman behind the information desk. She was the kind of perfectly groomed blonde that I generally equated with some corporate executive secretary. She looked up from her computer and hit me with a politely professional smile.

"And you are?"

"Harold White, a close friend of the family. I've been helping his grandmother with his medical oversight".

It wasn't exactly true, but it wasn't a total lie either. After all, she had told Doctor Anita that I could be given all information on his condition and treatments and I HAD been translating a lot of it for her. I figured it was worth a shot. Her perfectly manicured nails clicked against the keys as she typed a query into the computer on the desk.

"Mr. Raines is on the second floor, take the elevator to your left and when you get out on the second floor check in at the nurse's station to your right". Apparently dismissing me, she turned her attention back to the monitor in front of her.

Mentally shrugging I headed across the lobby to my left, towards a bank of elevators. When I glanced back I could see her screen. She was playing solitaire.

CHECKING IN AT THE nurse's station got me directions to Q's room and I found his grandmother sitting in a recliner next to the bed. She was holding his hand and talking quietly to him when I walked in.

A few hours in this new facility hadn't made a whole lot of difference but there were a couple of things I noticed immediately. First of all, he no longer appeared to have an IV running fluid into his hand.

Instead he had a plastic tube running into one side of his nose and taped to his cheek.

"Hi Mrs. Raines. How is he doing?"

She stood, even though I tried to convince her to stay in the chair. She did sit back down but not until she had given me a long, long hug. Why hadn't I ever noticed before how frail she was? That hug made me feel like I might snap her in two if I hugged too hard. Her frailty scared me a bit and I put a hand under her elbow to help her back into the chair.

She shook it off and snapped crossly at me, "Don't you go treating me like an old woman. I may not be young but I'm not going to break trying to get in and out of a chair".

That made me grin and I let it show. "Sorry about that. I guess I'm just hyper aware of everyone's mortality at this point".

"Humph..". was all I got for an answer so I looked back at Q for a moment.

"What do the doctor's in this place say?"

She took up Q's hand again. "Mostly they say that it's too early to tell anything. He will probably move to a different ward within a day or two. This one he is on right now is for new patients. They only stay here while the initial testing and evaluation is completed. Then they move to a different part of the building depending on what the tests show".

She finally looked up at me, "Did you know that they repeat every single test that they did over at St. Thomas? Apparently, they don't trust anybody else's methods and want to verify everything for themselves. They call it baselining, or something like that".

"Makes sense actually. Different machines can give slightly different results, depending on how they're calibrated. So, they probably want to use their own equipment in order to be sure that any changes they see later are real and not just the difference between the machines".

"That's exactly what the doctor here said", she beamed at me.

"What did the doctor say?" A heavily accented bass voice came from the doorway and I turned to see a tall black man who's voice instantly made me think of those old "Uncola" commercials from the 1980's.

I must have been staring because I nearly jumped when Mrs. Raines introduced the man.

"Harold, this is Doctor Hector Lamont. He's in charge of evaluating Quentin's condition".

The tall man reached out a hand to shake mine. A hand that seemed, to my 5 foot 5-inch perspective, to belong to a giant. He laughed at my expression and I found myself smiling even though I wasn't quite sure exactly what I was smiling about. He had that kind of infectious good humor that spilled over onto everyone around him and put them at ease.

"I'm pleased to meet you Harold. Mrs. Raines has spoken highly of you and tells me that you're far more likely to understand everything I say than she is...her words, not mine".

"Pleased to meet you Doctor Lamont. I apologize for staring at you when you walked in. You just look so familiar for some reason".

His laugh was what finally made it click. It seemed to come up from the depths of his soul and the bass thunder filled the room. "You are probably seeing my cousin...well, very distant cousin, to be sure. Apparently, I look and sound like him and since he was very famous, people tend to think they recognize me".

"Ah..". was all that came out and he laughed even harder.

"Relax my young friend. I assume you wish to know all there is to know about Quentin's condition, yes?"

"Um, yes. Of course". Mentally I kicked myself for being such a dolt. "Have you learned anything new?"

"Mostly we have spent the day confirming the information from the testing they did over at St. Thomas. Tomorrow we'll do some additional tests that we have developed ourselves and which we expect will give us a much more detailed picture of exactly what is going on with your friend. But we like to get the initial confirmation tests out of the way first. The next step starts with shaving his head". He ran one massive hand over his own polished, hairless skull for emphasis. "It will provide a much better contact for the EEG sensors and since our equipment here is much more sensitive, any way that we can improve the conductivity will only be to his benefit".

"Oh, right...that makes sense".

I glanced back at Q. He had always kept his hair short but somehow the idea of him being bald at eighteen seemed ludicrous. Or perhaps it was the doctor's contagious good humor, "If nothing else it must save a fortune in shampoo for your patients".

IT HAD BEEN DAYS SINCE I checked with RALPH to find out what he had learned. Between hanging out at the hospitals and spending hours monitoring the SPIDR feeds, I had been so busy that I had forgotten about asking him to research the cases of unexplained comas in recent months. As a result, it was a bit of a surprise to see his query on the screen when I got home.

'H, are you there?'

'Hello RALPH. Sorry I have been offline for so long.'

'Is your friend Q improving?'

'No, but he has some new doctors now. Did you find the information I requested?'

'Yes H. There have been 27 coma patients between the ages of 13 and 20 in the past 6 months within the greater New York City area. The breakout by cause follows:

Trauma (all types)-6

Anoxia due to diabetes-2

Drug overdose-12

Other/unknown-7

'What is the breakout by drug for the overdose cases?'
'The breakout of drug overdose by causative agent follows:
Unidentified-6 Heroin-3
Methamphetamines-2
Inhalants-1

That caught my attention. It was entirely possible that the 6 unidentified drug overdose cases were based on the same assumption that the cops had made about Toby Grey and Q. That would mean that there were actually 13 unknown cases in the past 6 months.

'RALPH, what is the total number of cases for the same period in each of the past 4 years?'

There was a short pause, only a few seconds, during which I assume RALPH was accessing multiple data systems to collect the data.

'The total for each of the past 4 years during the same 6-month window follows:
Yr. 1: Trauma-5; diabetic anoxia-3; Overdose-3; all others-3
Yr. 2: Trauma-8; diabetic anoxia-1; Overdose-5; all others-5
Yr. 3: Trauma-6; diabetic anoxia-1; Overdose-4; all others-4
Yr. 4: Trauma-5; diabetic anoxia-2; Overdose-2; all others-2

Well that was certainly strange. There was almost a threefold increase this year from the previous years.

'RALPH what is the explanation for the increase in the number of overdose and other cases this year?'

'Unknown'

I dropped backwards in my chair, my spine making a slight thump as I hit the hard spindles of the wooden chair. I wasn't sure exactly what I expected but that big of an increase most definitely had not been on my list.

Well, the police had been saying that a new drug was on the street, that it was at fault for all these cases and that was certainly plausible. Part of me wanted to say that I would have heard some rumors in school about a new drug but I knew that I would be lying to myself. I was a nerd, as uncool as they come. I was probably that last person in the city that anybody would talk to about illegal drugs.

CHAPTER 11

C arla
    "Why didn't they just arrest the scumbag?"

While I visited the Coma Research Center, Carla had been up in the spire of St. Peter the Redeemer monitoring the SPIDR feeds. She showed up at the apartment in a fury, stomping down the hallway with a face like a thunderstorm.

"I listened and the little prick is still free. I expected them to arrest him and interrogate him about the NEG. What the hell are they waiting for?"

I just sat there and let her vent. I could have tried to say something but it was easier to just let her get it out of her system first. Besides, I had questions and concerns of my own that I wanted to share. To be honest, I have always thought that Carla in a fury was pretty awe inspiring...not to mention downright hot.

Eventually she ran out of steam and just stood over me, glaring.

Hot...hot...hot. I crossed my legs and looked up at her.

"Well, you have to understand that they can't actually use any of the information we give them to make an arrest or get a conviction". I didn't get to say any more, she took off again.

"Then what have we been doing all this for? Why bother with the SPIDR and the surveillance, and the hours of listening to all the boring parts of their daily lives. C'mon H, what was the point, if they can't use it?"

I grinned up at her. "I never said they couldn't use it". She opened her mouth to say something but closed it with a snap, compressing her lips into a straight line and crossing her arms in front of her.

"I said they can't use it to make an arrest or get a conviction. Basically, what we did was illegal surveillance. Like tapping a phone without a court order. If they walked into a courtroom with our recording as evidence, the case would get thrown out and we would be accused of violating several kinds of privacy and due process laws".

I had looked those laws up before we started this whole game and what we had done was definitely illegal. That was the real reason that I was so adamant about being anonymous.

"I repeat", she was still glaring at me, "then what was the point?"

"Well, what they can do with the information is set a trap. They know exactly what is supposed to happen, when it's supposed to happen and who is supposed to do it. Complete with pictures of the gangster wanna-be. So, all they have to do is have plenty of surveillance at the scene, make sure that Officer Carson is wearing his bullet proof vest, and catch them in the act".

"Uh Huh, and isn't that kind of risky for officer Carson? What if he gets shot in the head instead of the torso?"

I spread my hands and shrugged. "Hey, we can't do all their thinking for them. We have to leave them some police work to do. Don't we?"

I got swatted for my pains.

"Anyway, I want to get your opinion on something else. Can you look at the data on my screen?" I waved at the laptop behind me and pushed myself up out of the chair, leaving it available to her. While she read the conversation between me and RALPH, I went to the kitchen and poured a couple of glasses of iced tea for us. When I put the sweating glass on the desk by the laptop, she looked up, her face grim.

THE ICE HAD LONG SINCE melted, turning the tea into thin brownish water. We had been arguing for more than an hour since Carla had read the information provided by RALPH. We agreed that it was a) circumstantial and b) intriguing. Beyond that, we were at opposite ends of the spectrum on what to do about it.

I wanted to do more research, see if we could discover a common factor. Carla, always more interested in the direct path to an objective, wanted to march into the Coma Center and demand that they provide more details and clarify exactly what was going on.

"Carla, think about what you're saying. You sound as if you're accusing them of deliberately putting people into comas. Why would they do that? What could they possibly have to gain?"

She flounced down on the edge of my bed, eyes flashing and hair fluffing out away from her head for a moment as she threw herself downward onto the mattress. I gritted my teeth.

"What makes you think that they know what's going on? It really could be that there is a new drug on the streets that's putting some kids into comas. C'mon", I grinned at her. "You have to admit that this one time, the cops might just be right".

"Yeah...sure...and the Apollo missions really were all just filmed in a Hollywood studio. Give me a break Harold".

Damn! She must really be annoyed because she never, ever, used my full name. She knew that I hated it and it would piss me off.

"Ockham's razor Carla".

"Yeah, yeah, I know...the simplest explanation is usually the right one. Fine, answer one question for me and I'll accept the premise that you could be right".

"OK".

"Can you honestly, in your heart and mind, believe that Q was taking drugs?"

I sagged back and surrendered. "No, you're right. I can't in my wildest nightmares believe that Q was experimenting with drugs. Especially with something unknown and new on the streets".

She sat up straight and stared me in the eye. "OK, then what does Ockham's razor say at this point?"

I sighed, "That there is some other cause. Something neither we nor the doctors are seeing".

————————————————————————

"NOW...EVERYTHING IN the cash drawer...hand it over!"

I ran the video back and played it through from the beginning. The central figure was a teenage male in a hoodie and jeans. His back was to the camera and he was holding a gun in his right hand, a gun aimed directly at Mr. Pak.

Well, to be more accurate, the gun aim wasn't really direct. The idiot was holding it up in the air, his arm fully extended above his head and the muzzle pointed down in more or less the direction of Mr. Pak. It was kind of hard to be sure of the exact aim because he kept waving it around for emphasis, stabbing down with it in Mr. Pak's direction. It looked exactly like something he must have seen in some movie and he probably thought it looked bad-ass and threatening. It might have at that, if you didn't realize that it's virtually impossible to actually aim a gun that way. On the other hand, from that distance, it was probably hard to miss hitting SOMETHING.

So, to other details, it was just the one guy and the camera aimed at the front door didn't show anybody outside. That meant that this was likely to be just some stupid punk who thought he could score some quick cash by robbing the Heavenly Delights Deli. There were however a few things wrong with that plan:

First, who robs a business at 10:30 in the morning? The place had only just opened so there really wasn't much in the register. All the fool got was the morning start up change.

Second, while the current camera angle didn't show his face, the high-definition camera we had built into the back of the cash register was pointed right at him, in glorious technicolor and 6million-pixel detail. Nor was the camera in the cash register the only one to get a really good view of the entire episode. There were six of them, all filming from different angles and distances.

Third, since he was alone and being very, very stupid about the whole thing, it meant that he probably wasn't a member of the NEG or any other gang so Mr. Pak could safely turn all the footage over to the police.

The security system had texted both Carla and me when the "no sale" key had triggered the video surveillance package that we had built for Mr. Pak. Overall, the whole setup had worked perfectly. I just kept wishing that Q had been there to see it.

CARLA SPENT THE NEXT afternoon at the Coma Center while I hid up in the church spire and watched as Officer Carson walked his beat.

From my perch, I had a hawk's eye view of the action and could clearly see the police cruisers stationed just up the side street from the intersection where the NEG candidate was supposed to make his move. I had been wondering how the police planned to have officer Carson walk his beat and still keep him alive. If they wanted to catch the gangbanger in the act or attempted act, it seemed to me that officer Carson was at some serious risk. After all, even if he was wearing a bullet proof vest, he could still be seriously injured or, if the bullet hit him in the head, he could be killed outright. Every cop in the city could be hiding around the corner but a lucky shot would still kill him.

Sweating, I watched as officer Carson and the gangster candidate closed the gap between them. I saw the kid raise his hand and start to point a pistol at the police officer. The next thing I saw was the gun fly out of the kid's hand and officer Carson pounce on him. In seconds, it was over and the kid was face down on the sidewalk with his hands cuffed behind his back. All those extra cops were converging on the scene but it didn't look as if they were going to be needed after all.

I had to run the recording back, play it in slow motion AND blow the image up to see what actually had happened. I hadn't been imagining things. The gun just flew out of the kid's hand, as if it was jerked away from him. Bemused, I played it back again, and then a third time. No matter how many times I watched it, the gun just seemed to fly away from him.

What my camera hadn't let me see was the police sniper in the other church spire.

When I realized that he was there and that it had been his shot that knocked the gun out of the kid's hand, I kind of freaked out for a bit. What if he had chosen this spire instead? I would have been caught up here and he might have arrested me as the kid's accomplice!

While I was watching, the police do their thing, Carla was visiting Q and his grandmother at the

Coma Center. I got a text message from her just as I was getting home that evening.

"Found link. Meet before class"

CHAPTER 12

Where in the world is Carla Pak?

Carla wasn't in school the next day and I was on pins and needles all day, wondering where she was. On the way home I stopped at the Heavenly Delights Deli. The doors were locked and the lights were out.

What the hell?

I had texted her about 6 times without getting an answer and I was still standing there on the sidewalk when one of neighbors walked past. She stopped and turned back to me.

"They're closed".

"Yeah, I see that. Any idea why?"

"I'm not sure what happened exactly but early this morning an ambulance was here and I saw them load the daughter into it".

I stared at the woman in shock. Don't say it...please don't say it.

Apparently glad to be able to pass on a juicy tidbit she leaned towards me slightly, a smug expression, "Looked to me like she was unconscious. Teenagers these days. Bet it was a drug overdose. Always did think that little miss goody two-shoes was too perfect".

Oh hell! I knew it wasn't drugs but decided that trying to convince the old busybody would be pointless. I walked away without acknowledging her words.

I WANTED MORE THAN anything to head to the hospital but

I couldn't. For one thing, I couldn't be one hundred percent sure which hospital she was taken to. It was probably St. Francis but if they were overloaded, it could have been any one of several others in the city. It made more sense to try to find out for sure first rather than just run willy nilly all over the place, trying to find the right one.

I knew mom was working and wouldn't be home for several more hours but that was OK. I walked in the door and headed directly to my laptop. I logged directly in the BEC system and queried RALPH.

'RALPH, are you online?' 'Of course H. How are you today?' 'Fine RALPH but I need your help".

'How can I help you H?'

'I need to do two pieces of research. The first is to find the most recent teenage coma patient. I'm pretty sure there was one this morning'.

There was a short hesitation.

'Yes H, there was a teenage female admitted to St. Francis today in a coma. How did you know that there was a new case?'

'The patient, Carla Pak is a close friend of mine'.

'I'm sorry to hear about your friend. What is your second query?'

'Last night I received a text from Carla that she had figured out how the unexplained comas were related. I need your help to find out what that connection is'.

'How do we find that H? I do not see any obvious connection between the patients'.

I spent a couple of hours online with RALPH but didn't come up with anything that seemed to connect the victims or their cases. Other than the obvious fact that they were all teenagers they were all different sexes, ages, schools, racial backgrounds, social status, and history. According to RALPH the data was widely diverse in all areas without any particular areas of overlap.

I found myself wondering what Carla had figured out that eluded a serious artificial intelligence and a guy with an IQ two points higher than Einstein...supposedly.

In the end, I gave up and headed over St. Francis to check on Carla, if I could.

IT TOOK ME A WHILE to reach the ICU, which is where they had Carla. When I did get there, I was met by Mr. Pak and his wife Maria, in the company of a plain clothes police officer. I found out fairly fast that he was a detective and was assigned to the same task I had just been working on...figuring out what was happening to the city's teenagers.

"So, I understand that you're close to the two most recent victims, Mr...?" "H".

"Mr. H? You think you're in some B-rate spy flick, do you son?"

I shook my head in denial and Mrs. Pak interjected.

"He doesn't like Harold so he always goes by H".

"Thanks Mrs. Pak".

She patted me on the arm, "Just tell the officer anything you can think of that might help, won't you Harold?"

"Sure Mrs. Pak. Sure". I turned back to the detective. "Not making jokes sir. As she said, that's just what everyone calls me".

"Sorry. This case is making me edgy. I have a teenage daughter of my own and if there is some new drug on the street, I want it gone before she gets hurt by it".

"Yeah, I get it. Anyway, to answer your question. Yes, both Carla and Q... Quentin Raines, sorry; they are my two closest friends. I swear to you officer, those two never touched any drugs. I would bet my life on it".

"You could be doing just that kid. If there is something new out there and kids that normally don't use drugs are getting it, how the hell is anybody safe?"

It was a good question. It was also the same one that had been running around and around in my head like a hamster in a wheel. The hamster did a couple more quick laps and I finally got an idea.

"I wish I could help you. I really do. Unfortunately, I'm not exactly a social butterfly. Being a nerd, I'm on the low end of the social totem pole and probably the last person in the whole New York City school system that would hear about some new drug. I only even know about three cases. Are you saying there are more?"

He did not answer my question. Instead he squinted down at me and snapped a different question altogether.

"Wait...you know THREE of the victims? Who is the third one?"

"Huh? Oh, Toby Grey".

"...and just what is your relationship to Mr. Grey?" He was seriously starting to look at me as if I were a tasty morsel and I suddenly realized what he must be thinking. I started to sweat and waved my hands in front of me, palms out as if warding off an attack.

"Um, I don't have any kind of relationship with Toby Grey. I don't actually know him at all. I only know that he is in this same kind of coma and I only know that because Carla is friends with Toby's girlfriend. Carla kept her company for a few days right after he landed in the hospital and told us all about it".

"And just who is "us"? He scowled at me even harder.

"Q... Quentin Raines and me. We have been close to Carla since the three of us were kids".

"And you have no idea what the any of them might have taken?"

"No". I was starting to get annoyed. "As far as I know, none of them ever tried any kind of drug. Never. Maybe somebody slipped them something". I shook my head, "except that I can't imagine any reason why somebody would drug three high school honor students".

"Honor Students? All three of them?"

"Well, I know Carla and Q are and I'm pretty sure about Toby Grey as well. I remember Q saying that he ran up against Toby at the FIRST competition a year or so back".

"The first competition?" the detective had been scribbling notes in a little flip pad but looked up as he asked the question.

"F.I.R.S.T, it's an international robotics competition for high school students that happens every year. It runs for months and having a winning team can pretty much guarantee you get into any first-rate college you want".

"So... anybody keen enough to win, that they might try to eliminate the competition?"

Damn, I hadn't thought of that! I wondered briefly if that was the link that Carla had found but it seemed pretty weak. I knew a few participants from previous years who had been ticked off about losing but Carla never participated and Q hadn't been on a winning team. He probably could have won on his own, but the team structure paired him with others who weren't exactly up to his level of mechanical engineering genius.

"Competition is tight but not that tight. I can't think of anybody who is so hard over to win that they would be trying to kill off the competition. Even if that were the case, why give...whatever it is to Carla? I know she never participated in the FIRST competitions and I don't remember her mentioning it for this year either".

"Hmm. Well the honor student thing is the only link I have between the various victims so far, unless you want to count living in the greater New York City area. If being bright is the only common factor, then it might be worth investigating that angle. I'm sure that it's probably just these three, but it won't hurt to run a quick inquiry into the academic history of all the victims".

He nodded and seemed about to leave. I reached out and touched his arm.

"Detective, will you let me know if that turns out to be a true link?"

"Why?" his voice was flat and a bit suspicious.

"Because I have a higher IQ than either Carla or Q. If somebody is targeting the smart students,

I'm probably on their list. I would really like to know whether I need to worry about that or not".

"Kid, if I were you, I would worry anyway. Something is happening to these kids and we don't have the foggiest idea what it is. If you're all that smart, that should worry you. No matter what the connection is".

He left and almost immediately, Doctor Juarez came striding into the room. I ended up having almost exactly the same conversation all over again with her. The difference was that she wasn't looking for a perpetrator, she just seemed to want to help Carla. It was a distinction I appreciated.

CHAPTER 13

New Recruits
　　With Carla and Q both out of it, I wasn't going to be able to keep everything going. I was trying to do way too many things at once, including:

Visiting with Q at the JECRC,

Visiting Carla at the St. Francis Intensive Care Unit,

Monitoring things at the NEG,

Monitoring things at the Heavenly Delights Deli,

Going to school,

Doing homework for NEG members to avoid pain,

Trying to research the connection between the coma cases

There is no way I could continue to juggle all that and stay sane. I was going to need help. I ended up recruiting a few others from school to help with different parts of the security and NEG projects.

I started the next morning with Roger Barksdale. He was a huge bruiser of a guy who didn't have many brains but did have plenty of brawn. His Nordic blond hair and blue eyes might have been attractive but the fact that he had basically no neck and had muscles on his muscles just made him intimidating. I needed somebody to respond to the deli if the security system went off. Preferably somebody big and bad enough looking to help put a stop to things before they went too far. If not that, then at least to loom menacingly after the fact so that nobody disturbed Mr.

Pak while he inventoried the damage and called the cops. He was also big enough that even the NEG didn't usually bother him, but he knew most of them by sight and could tell Mr. Pak if the NEG was involved.

I couldn't afford to pay him for the job but he had a different idea anyway. His family owned a dry-cleaning shop up the block and he wanted the same security system installed there. In return, he would watch over both places and respond if needed.

I didn't really have the time for it but needed the help so I spent the weekend upgrading their ancient cash register and installing cameras. I used Roger instead of a ladder to install the ones near the ceiling, which was nice since I'm not a huge fan of ladders at the best of times.

I also recruited two girls from the computer science class to help with monitoring the SPIDR records and identifying anything interesting or (more importantly) incriminating. Keisha and Danae were both certifiable computer geniuses so they didn't take long to understand the system and they both liked the idea of belonging to a group that was taking the security and safety of the area in hand. I had to promise a security system to Keisha's family business as well but needed Q back to help with manufacturing more micro-cams and SPIDRs. Without that, I was going to have to find somebody who could reverse engineer what Q had done. That wasn't going to be easy.

The four of us met up at the deli the first afternoon and all of them wanted to know what the rules were and if the group had a name. Apparently, they thought that Q, Carla, and I had formed some sort of gang or club. Rather than argue, I thought for a second and gave them a name...the Golden Horde.

Not that the four of us constituted a horde, but it had a nice ring to it and historically it was kind of cool. The Golden Horde was the name used for the Mongols who had controlled most of what is now Russia and it had been run by one of Genghis Khan's younger sons. During his reign, the Golden Horde had been the light of Asia, an organization that codified laws, ushered in an era of prosperity, and promoted scientific discoveries. For a group of brainiacs trying to do something good with technology, it seemed fitting.

To be perfectly honest, it also sounded kind of bad ass, in a highbrow kind of way. I was sort of proud that I dreamed it up off the top of my head. As for rules, I promised them copies of those would be provided the next day so that they could learn them. "Is there any kind of initiation ceremony?" Jeez, what had I gotten myself into?

"Of course, but under the circumstances, with both Carla and Q out of commission, I hereby waive the initiation ceremony requirement. You will, of course be required to memorize the rules and swear fealty to the Golden Horde, in due time".

Roger raised his hand. I swear, he must have thought he was in class or something. Did I mention that he really isn't all that bright?

"Yes Roger?"

"Um....what does fealty mean?"

I growled a bit and he looked taken aback, which was kind of funny since he could have pulverized me with one blow. "Ah...it means you have to swear to be loyal to the Golden Horde, and to follow orders".

He nodded, his face serious, while the girls smirked.

"Sure, that makes sense".

Apparently following orders was something that he felt capable of.

HAVING APPARENTLY FORMED some kind of covert street gang and set up Carla, Q, and myself as the titular heads of the thing, I ran with it. Honestly, I wasn't sure what else I could do. I was pretty sure the girls thought it was all just good fun but Roger seemed to need the structure, and I needed Roger. So, there you have it. We were a horde...or at least a gang...of four.

Now all I had to do was create a set of rules for the horde and we would be in business. I sat up late that night, browsing the internet for gang rules, creeds, whatever; and creating a set for the golden horde. I ended up borrowing heavily from Buddha, The Bushido code, fifteenth century knightly vows and a dozen other sources. Once I mashed them all together what I got was:

1. I will refrain from causing harm and taking life, both human and non-human, except to preserve life from injustice or evil.
2. I will not steal, tell lies, or otherwise attempt to gain anything not rightfully mine
3. I will not engage in illegal activities unless they are necessary to preserve the health and life of those around me.

1. I will always try to act with integrity and honesty in all things.
2. I will not turn a blind eye to injustice or to those who cause pain to others.
3. I will respect all members of the Golden Horde as my family.
4. I will not discriminate against others due to race, color, creed, religion, abilities, life choices, or other reasons; but will always attempt to be supportive of those around me in their lives and choices, so long as those choices do not discriminate against others or violate any of the rules of the Golden Horde
5. What occurs between any people by mutual consent, is acceptable as long as it does not harm others.
6. I'm responsible for everything I do or say and accept freely the consequences that follow both my words and actions.
7. The purpose of the Golden Horde is to provide protection to our members and their families. If necessary, the Golden Horde will take action against other gangs or organizations that threaten members and their families.
8. I will not divulge the secrets of the Golden Horde to non-members without the approval of the leadership.

It all felt a bit hokey and grandiose but what can I say, it made sense to me and seemed to make our little horde feel real. Like it might do something good along the way.

DANAE BROUGHT BILLY Nedset into the horde, after talking to me about him. Billy attended a magnet school for gifted teens and was a peripheral friend of Q's. They had a friendly competition that had run for years through a series of science fairs and academic competitions. The upside was that Billy was nearly the equal of Q when it came to mechanical engineering...nearly.

I reluctantly surrendered one of the five remaining original SPIDRs to him for reverse engineering. I wasn't sure if he could do it and I don't think he was sure either. With Q out of commission, we were going to need to be able to create more of them eventually. Billy was our best hope of doing that.

Looking at our happy little horde, the only thing that all five of us had in common was that we lived in a relatively close area. On the upside for me personally was that Roger was generally able to join me on the walk to and from school. My stomach settled down a lot when I didn't have to stress so much over trying to sneak through NEG territory twice every day.

So, the horde had its course laid out and I could settle into the serious business of trying to retrace Carla's last day so that I could figure out what it was that she had seen or heard that resulted in her landing in the Intensive Care Unit at St. Francis Hospital. Several conversations with RALPH as well as Billy, Keisha, and Danae had made it clear that we all thought the same thing. Somebody was deliberately causing people, specifically teenagers, to fall into persistent comas. We had the what, but the who, when, where, why, and how were all a blank.

There was one other negative that week. The NEG had failed to kill Officer Carson but had severely beaten a couple of tourists who had wandered down the wrong street. Arika hadn't been involved, or she hadn't worn the SPIDR earrings that day. Either way we didn't have any solid evidence that we could pass to the police. A couple of days later one of the tourists had died.

CHAPTER 14

A Bug-Eyed view
The next time I went to visit Q he had been moved to a new room on a different floor. He also had a new doctor. Apparently, Doctor Lamont oversaw evaluating all new admissions to the program but didn't generally do their ongoing care. I jolted to a halt two steps inside the door to Q's room.

He was lying on the bed wearing what looked like one of those old rubber swim caps, except that it was snug to his freshly shaved skull. It had tiny buttons covering almost every square millimeter of the surface. The last time I saw him, there had been a couple of dozen wires pasted to his head and running to a recording machine that perched on the bedside table. This new cap didn't have any wires.

His grandmother wasn't in the room either. I walked over and sat in the big chair next to the bed, trying to figure out what to say to him. I've always read that people in a coma can hear you and when or if they wake up, sometimes they even remember hearing conversations going on around them. The topic had always been totally academic before and now, faced with this silent, unresponsive body in the bed, I wondered if he really could hear anything. More than that, I wondered if he was actually in there at all, or if the Q I had known for so many years was simply gone forever. Dead but with a body that was too stupid to know it was dead or too smart to stop performing its normal functions. I found myself talking to him anyway, just in case.

"Hey Q". I paused, totally unprepared and with no idea of what to say next.

I ended up spending a couple of hours there, sitting next to the bed and telling Q everything that had happened since finding him lying on his bedroom floor. I explained about the police thinking it was some new street drug and how Carla and I didn't believe he was doing drugs. I told the story of tipping off the police about the hit on Officer Carson and how Carla was in the same ICU, with the same problem, where he had been under the care of Doctor Anita Juarez. I waxed eloquent about Doctor Anita; how attractive she was and how much she seemed to care about what was happening to my friends. Finally, I told him about the creation of the Golden Horde.

"Q, you would have laughed yourself silly if you had been there. The three of them were so solemn and so into the whole concept. Roger is the most dedicated of the three. I know that we never thought very highly of him because he isn't all that bright. But I have a feeling about him, Q. I think that he has been just as much of an outsider as we have, but for the exact opposite reason. I also think that he will be intensely loyal to the Horde". I couldn't hold back my own laughter at that point. "A horde...of five now. Seven if you and Carla wake back up".

I paused in my story telling and wiped my eyes, for what seemed like the hundredth time.

"You've gotta wake up Q. I need you and your grandmother needs you. She's here all the time. We have to make her go home to rest occasionally and even then; she doesn't stay there very long. I think the apartment without you is just too empty for her to cope with. I mean, it must be kind of spooky there alone, especially knowing that you're here. This is a great facility though. I looked them up and they have really great success with coma patients. I think they can help you here...I really do".

I lingered a bit longer and was walking through the lobby on my way out when there was a commotion at the main doors. I peeked around the corner and saw them bringing a patient in from an ambulance. I couldn't see who it was at first because there was a whole crowd of white lab coats clustered around the stretcher as it rolled across the open space. When they passed me, I caught a glimpse of a still female figure, face partially covered by an oxygen mask. I was half afraid that it was Carla but I didn't know the teenage blonde girl I could see between the white coats.

THE SIGHT OF YET ANOTHER teenage patient being brought to the JECRC freaked me out and I ended up back over at St. Francis to see Carla. I just had this overwhelming urge to check up on her. There wasn't any change, of course. After visiting her and her parents for a bit, I headed home. I needed to do some more research.

Days passed and nothing changed. Eventually Carla was moved from St. Francis Hospital to the JECRC. I was there when they made the move this time and found myself helping the staff collect all her personal stuff from the room. I picked up the plastic bag of the things Carla had with her when she had arrived in the hospital and headed for the elevator when one of the nurses caught up with me. She held out a pair of earrings and handed them to me.

"Here, she was wearing these when she came in. We had to take them off when we hooked up the EEG leads".

I accepted them from her and thanked her for all she and the rest of the staff had done for both Carla and Q. As she turned away I looked more closely at the earrings and finally realized why we had only gotten data from one of Arika's SPIDR earrings. She had only been wearing one. Carla must have split the pair and given Arika one SPIDR and one similar earring. An earring that was purely decorative but looked like its smarter partner. The other one was in my hand.

As amazing as those little SPIDRs were, I found myself frustrated by the fact that they only broadcast but didn't have a record function. If they had been able to record, I might have been able to simply play the thing back and find out what Carla had seen or heard the night she had sent me that text. When Q wakes up, I'll have to talk to him about a recording option for his little critters. The thought popped into my head and I stopped dead in my tracks, realizing that he might never wake up. I might have lost my best friend; lost him forever.

SEVERAL THINGS BROKE loose at the same time that Saturday. Keisha and Danae caught a break with the recordings on the laptop and picked up a conversation about plans to distribute both marijuana and crack to students at the high school. There was enough detail in it to warrant another information drop to the police.

This time we used the original plan. The girls went uptown and dropped the envelop into a mail slot in one of the hotels. There was apparently a whole week before the NEG was expecting delivery of the drugs so there was plenty of time, even for the United States Post Office to get the letter delivered. This time it was sent to the attention of Captain Payne at the precinct station because part of the plan was never to deliver to the same officer twice and by preference we would have them delivered to different stations in the future as well.

While all this was going on, Roger got a page from his parent's new security system and arrived in time to thwart a couple of NEG toughs who were causing trouble. They hadn't really seemed to want to steal anything this time; instead they were intent upon just causing mischief and instilling fear into the locals. Unfortunately for them, Roger rounded up a couple of friends from the wrestling team and brought them with him. The three of them must have made a truly impressive wall of muscle because the gangers saw them and beat a hasty retreat from his parent's shop.

Roger's parents were ecstatic about having the trouble stopped early and suddenly the Golden Horde was a popular secret on the street. Publicity wasn't really what I had in mind, but I suppose people were bound to find out what we were doing sooner or later. I found myself wishing for later but the universe apparently decided that sooner was more appropriate. I didn't have to like it, just roll with it.

We started to get requests from other businesses in area for security systems. Most were willing to pay us pretty decent money to augment their existing systems or even replace them outright. Unfortunately, Q wasn't around to make any more SPIDRs and Billy was still working on the reverse engineering project. We did make good use of micro-cameras that we bought online. We got deposits from a couple of businesses in advance and used the money to pay for the cameras and to get things set up.

KEISHA LIVES IN AN elegant old townhouse that borders on the verge of NEG territory. It also sits just two houses from the St. Peter the Redeemer church. Sunday afternoon the entire Horde was gathered in the basement to work. Even though we were all in one place, we were all working independently.

We had taken over her father's man cave since he was out of town for a couple of weeks on some business trip. He was a lawyer for some multi-national corporation and traveled a lot of the time. Using his cave gave us a great place to work and total privacy. It was also a LOT more comfortable than the deli or library at school. Roger hadn't really seemed very happy to be in the library with us so this was better for him as well.

Roger was in the corner using a weight set and universal gym that belonged to Keisha's dad. The occasional clanks and thumps constituted most of the sound in the room and were oddly comforting. I don't know, perhaps my brain translated the sounds into an assurance that large, strong muscles were nearby if I needed protection. Not that there was anything in that house to hurt any of us, but skinny little teenage nerds tend to feel unsafe a lot of the time.

Keisha was monitoring the SPIDR feeds. She had gotten tired of climbing up all those stairs in the church spire and sitting in the grubby room at the top for hours to watch the video recordings. She had solved the problem by the simple expedient of swapping the external hard drive out and bringing the full one home. Working at home meant she could be a lot more comfortable even if it did lack the occasional background concert from the pipe organ. She sat across the card table from me, headphones on, soda in one hand and the other petting the svelte orange tabby sleeping in her lap.

The tabby was named Sher Khan but generally just called Khan and it was the most amazing house cat I have ever met. It was the deep orange of a ginger cat but had the dark gray/brown stripes of a tabby. The end result was a cat that looked a lot like a miniature tiger. When I had first arrived at the house, the cat had sauntered over and sat just out of reach, squinting up at me as if examining my soul for defects. I stretched out one finger in his direction and he leaned forward slightly to touch his nose to it. Apparently satisfied that I wasn't some evil intruder, he had turned his back on me and returned to the lap of his primary human minion, namely Keisha.

Billy was using a projects workbench on one side of the room. Apparently, Keisha's dad dabbled in a lot of different projects and was a bit of a general fix-it man for small appliances and electronic devices. Nothing nearly as sophisticated as the stuff that Billy and Q normally worked on, but it meant that he had a workbench and many of the right kinds of tools. Those tools included a lamp with an articulating arm and a huge built-in magnifying glass. At the moment, he was using the lens to help him see the guts of the SPIDR that he was dissecting.

Danae was stretched on the sofa with her laptop perched on a tray across her thighs. She was working on some scanning code to prescreen the SPIDR video for key words and images, hoping to drastically reduce the number of hours we had to spend reviewing the stuff by hand. I had introduced her to RALPH and the two of them were collaborating on the work.

Now, I know that RALPH is a computer program and not a real person. Even though I know that intellectually, there was a part of me that was just a teensy bit jealous of how well they seemed to work together. Dumb, but there it is. It seems that I'm human after all.

"Hey guys, check this out". Keisha grabbed a remote control and turned on the sixty-inch flat screen TV that hung on the far wall. A few key taps and the feed from her laptop was running on the TV in high definition and surround sound.

On the screen were several members of the NEG. From the angle, we must have been watching one of the static SPIDRs that had been sent in through a cracked window and was hiding up near the ceiling of the room.

One big guy with his head shaved down to a dark fuzz and tattoos all around his neck was surrounded by a half dozen others, mostly male but a couple of girls were there as well. The big guy grabbed one of the girls by the back of the neck and shoved her face down on the ground. The other girl dragged the girl's skirt up (it was pretty short and didn't have to move far) and her panties down.

"Oops!" the screen went dark. "Sorry, that wasn't the part I wanted to show".

"What the Hell was that?" I blurted it out before my brain caught up and told me the obvious.

It was Danae that answered, "Looks like a new girl getting jumped into the NEG".

Both Billy and Roger looked as unsettled as I felt. Oddly, the girls didn't seem as shocked as we did. "You mean that girls who join gangs have to...", Roger didn't finish the sentence.

Keisha looked from one to the other of us with a rather bland expression, "How did you think girls got initiated?"

"Gangs are all about power and control. Sex is one of the primary ways that men have always exerted power and control over women". Danae seemed unmoved as well. "Don't any of you pay any attention in history class at all? Ever hear of the Droit du Seigneur?"

Roger surprised me by being the one to answer, "Doesn't that mean the Lord's Right?"

She smiled at him in approval. "Yes, it does Roger. But specifically, what it meant was that in ancient and medieval times, a local lord had the right to bed any virgin he wanted. Preferably on her wedding night, before her new husband got anywhere near her".

Keisha chimed in, "It makes sense, from a genetic view. It was a way for the most noble, and therefore presumably the best and strongest, to propagate their own genes as widely as possible. Very Darwinian in fact. You know, the DNA of the strongest and most fit is more likely to be spread through the population that way".

I was really feeling uncomfortable with the matter-of-fact way the girls were discussing the whole concept. Not so much like they approved, but that they accepted it on a scientific level as a basic fact of life.

"Virgins were also less likely to have any disease that they might pass to their lord".

"Very true Billy".

I couldn't stand listening to it any more. "Am I the only one that finds this totally horrifying and disgusting?"

The girls looked at me pityingly. "Not being a girl, it isn't something you've ever had to confront. For us, it's a simple fact of existence...there are guys out there that get their jollies by raping girls. Whether that occurs one-on-one in a dark alley or in a group setting like the NEG, that's just geography. It's all the same thing in the end. Just the male of the species trying to spread his own DNA as far and wide as he can. Any way he can. These guys", she waved a hand at the TV, "have just found a way to institutionalize it".

I changed the topic slightly, "Can the cops use this as evidence?"

Keisha shook her head doubtfully. "Even if the girl would press charges, it's still illegally obtained video. And she won't testify if she was being jumped in because then it was voluntary. They might be able to get a couple of the older ones on statutory rape charges, depending on how old she is. But she looks like she's close to seventeen which makes her old enough to legally consent in this state".

"It would also be easy to find the SPIDR and destroy it, if anybody connected with the NEG saw the video. The angle is pretty obvious".

I shuddered hard and took a deep breath to clear the images from my brain. "So, we can't do anything about that?" Both girls shook their heads so I decided to move on. "What was it you wanted to show us Keisha?"

KEISHA PULLED UP ANOTHER section of video and transferred it to the TV. It appeared to be taking place sometime later than the first scene. The two girls were still there, the one who was jumped into the gang looked a good deal worse for the wear but wasn't crying. The older girl stood close with her arm around the younger one's shoulders, looking like a proud mama whose daughter had just won a prize. I felt sick. The guys in the image appeared to have forgotten the girls and the recent events.

"Jorge, you got the information?" The speaker was tall, slender, and almost eloquent in his movements. His thick hair fell just to chin level in deep waves that were almost feminine. He also sported several expensive looking rings on each hand. Unlike the rest of the gang members, he did not appear to have any tattoos. At least none that were visible on camera.

Jorge on the other hand appeared to be an average sized Latino with a spiderweb tattooed on one side of his neck and a gold hoop in his left earlobe. He made H think of pirates, all he was missing was a puffy sleeve shirt and a cutlass.

"Yeah boss, I got it". He pulled a folded piece of paper from his shirt pocket and opened it up, pressing it flat on the table surface. "Just like the man promised".

The Boss put his hand on Jorge's shoulder, giving it an approving squeeze. "I knew I could count on you Jorge. You've always been my right hand".

The two of them bent over the page and read silently.

When they were done, the leader straightened and looked around the room, eyes lingering on each person in turn. He finally settled on a skinny youth with bad skin and a sallow complexion that made him look like an extra from a zombie film. "Aaron".

The kid jumped slightly as if he had been goosed by somebody behind him. "Yah boss?" He did not look eager for whatever was coming.

"Your next target is a student from your school. His name is Harold". He consulted the piece of paper again. "Harold White".

I stared at the screen; my mind frozen along with my body. I was a target? A target of the NEG? It made no sense. I had almost no contact with anybody in the NEG, with the exception of Karl and one other kid who got their term papers from me. Certainly, I hadn't done anything to draw their anger. Nothing at all, unless they had figured out about the SPIDR. If they had, then why was the one we were watching from still working? I struggled to pay attention to what was happening on the screen but my brain didn't seem to function right anymore.

"Keisha, can you back that up a bit? To just after he said my name". It sounded strange in my own head and even stranger out loud.

She ran it back and froze it at that point. She left it frozen and waited for me to collect myself and draw a circle in the air with one hand to indicate that she should continue the playback. The skinny kid was talking.

"Like the last two? Won't it look strange, three in a row from the same school?"

The boss shook his head as he spoke, denying the logic. "Nah, the cops are still following the trail of a new designer drug". He smirked as he spoke, "From their point of view, what could be more logical than three friends all taking the same drug?"

"I dunno, but if it was me, I would be wondering why the third one would try it when he already knew what it did to his two friends. I think it would be damned odd for him to go ahead anyway after they both ended up as vegetables".

"Well...you might be right. But you have your orders. Get it done by the end of the week. Or you can take his place".

The skinny kid gulped and nodded vigorously. "Sure thing, I can do it, no problem". He was babbling by that point, "no problem at all".

CHAPTER 15

Now what?

The argument lasted over an hour.

Danae and Billy wanted to take the video to the police and have them put me in protective custody or something.

"This is out of our league and you know it". Billy kept saying over and over, "We can't take on the NEG. It would be suicide. Besides, what could we do to them on our own? We should just take this video to the police and let them handle it. They have people who are trained to deal with this kind of thing".

"Humph! Really? They have people trained to handle gangbangers who go around causing people to fall into comas that the doctors can't explain and can't stop? Which chapter of the New York Police Department training manual do you think that falls under?" Keisha's voice dripped sarcasm.

Billy opened his mouth to retort but closed it again when he realized that he couldn't think of any kind of comeback.

Keisha on the other hand, wanted to handle things ourselves and avoid official entanglements.

"So, we take our illegally obtained evidence to the cops and they arrest us for violating the

NEG's privacy, illegal wiretapping, and fourteen other violations of the National Security Statutes". She threw her hands up in despair. "Ever looked up what happens in protective custody? You get thrown in the same prison as the criminals. But you get solitary confinement.

They get more freedoms in there than you do. How is that fair or reasonable?"

Danae wrinkled her brow as she tried to think of a legal alternative. "What about the witness protection program?

Couldn't they protect H that way?"

'Sure, they can take him away from his mother and all of us. Give him a new name and new identity in a different part of the country. Then they would forbid him to ever have contact of any kind with Q, Carla, all of us, or anybody else even remotely connected with the case. Answer a couple of questions for me". Keisha was sneering, her gaze roving from one person to the next and making everyone squirm, even me. "How do you expect him to ever get his life back if he can't investigate what is going on? More importantly, what kind of solution is it to tear him away from his own life and force him to live in hiding when it's the NEG that's doing something wrong, not H?"

None of us had any kind of immediate answer for that.

Roger, being the more direct type, just wanted to hunt down the skinny kid and pound on him until he told us every detail of what was going on and exactly what he had done to Q and Carla.

Not to mention, of course, telling us who the dandy was and who was calling the shots.

I must admit that Roger's solution held a certain appeal. The moment I had realized that the skinny kid (what was his name...oh yeah, Aaron) had been involved in whatever had happened to Q and Carla, not to mention Toby and all the other teens who were now lying unconscious, heads shaved and hooked up to machines so that their bodies would continue to function. As soon as that realization hit me, I wanted to find the little runt and do some pounding of my own. So, I was definitely able to sympathize with Roger's view.

I let the bickering go on for a few more minutes while I considered my options. Finally, I couldn't stand it anymore.

"That's enough!"

The room fell silent as four pairs of eyes turned in my direction, uniformly wide with surprise.

"That's enough", I repeated more softly when I had everybody's attention. "I'm not going to let the authorities put me in the witness protection program. First of all, that program is for people who can testify that they actually saw a crime being committed...which I haven't. I know exactly as much as the rest of you at this point. So... unless all five of us are going into Witness

Protection, there is no point in any one of us doing it".

I paused for a breath but continued rapidly, because I saw mouths start to open to respond to my declaration.

"As for protective custody. That's not happening either. If I'm in a cell someplace, then I can't help Q, or Carla, or anybody else. Not to mention that we still have no idea WHY I'm their current target or why any of the others were chosen either, for that matter. I won't allow myself to be locked away where I can't do anything to help resolve the situation. Nor will I sit around in a jail cell while I wait for the police to figure out what is going on. I could be old and gray before that happens".

"So, what do you want to do then?" Danae, who had been the quietest throughout the whole argument, finally spoke.

"Well, part of me really finds Roger's plan appealing". I shook my head in negation before the torrent of replies could get started. "But I won't let these petty hoods drive me down to their own level by involving violence. No, the Golden Horde may intimidate people". I grinned at Roger to soothe his ruffled feathers. "But we don't stoop to their level. Not unless forced to it in self-defense".

I shifted in my chair, sitting up straight and gazing around at them, pausing to pin each one with my gaze before continuing.

"What we're going to do is fight them with our brains as well as brawn".

"Billy, I need those new SPIDRs, or something else that we can use to collect information. If you don't have the reverse engineering on the SPIDR ready, can you rig up some other kind of bugging device for us? Something we can slip into backpacks, or attach to clothing somehow?"

He took a long moment to think on it before answering, "I can either work on the SPIDR or I can work on generating something simpler for the short term. I can't do both at the same time".

"How long do you think you need for the SPIDR?"

He took a deep breath and blew it out before answering, stalling for time to think. "Probably a couple of weeks, minimum. Maybe longer".

"OK, drop them for now. Focus on something we can use to bug skinny Aaron directly".

"Ok".

I turned to the girls, looking to Danae first. "You are going to have a lot more data to review. Can you work with Keisha on the software to scan for key elements?" She nodded and I turned to

Keisha.

"How long to have something up and running?"

She looked upset and I wasn't sure why. "I have a basic program available now, but it's only scanning audio for key words. I need you to verify the word list before I put it in production.

Imaging will take a couple of more days, I think".

"Work with RALPH on that part, can you?"

She brightened a bit and that earlier stab of jealousy popped up in my back brain again. I shook it away and went on.

"What about me?" Roger had walked across the room, swung a chair around backwards and straddled it, arms across the top of the chair back. Now he looked like a kid being told he was going to miss Christmas. I grinned and pointed one finger at him, my hand cocked as if the finger was a gun.

"You, have one of the most important tasks. You keep me alive and safe while we figure out what's going on. I trust you more than the cops to keep Aaron and his cronies away from me".

"Can I pound him if he gets too close?"

I patted him on the arm in consolation. "Only if he makes a move to hurt me. Mostly I want you to loom threateningly at anybody that looks as if they want to cause trouble or hurt any of us...especially me".

"O-kay. But look H, I can't be awake and with you all the time. We aren't in the same classes for one thing. Not to mention that I'm going to have to sleep sometimes".

I nodded in agreement but kept quiet because he seemed to have a solution in mind. I know that the rest of us brainiacs could be a little intimidating to Roger and wanted to encourage him to solve things whenever possible.

"Can I bring in some of the guys from the wrestling team? If we had more muscle available, we could do a better job of protecting you. I figure that the job is going to be bigger than it should be. Cause for all your brains, you aren't gonna do the smart thing and lie low...are you?"

"Probably not". I considered his suggestion. "You got anybody in particular in mind and are you suggesting asking them for help just with this or bringing them in all the way...making them real members of the Golden Horde?"

I had the feeling that the Horde was working its way to being one in truth and not just in name and wondered how big it would get. It was still a really strange sensation to realize that I was the leader of this weird group.

"I think". He paused as if to emphasis the point. "I think we should bring them all the way in, if they are willing". He waved his hands as he spoke, clearly finding a passion for his subject. "Look, these guys are like me. They are big and strong but not always too bright. Oh, sure, there are some real smart guys on the wrestling team but they aren't the ones I'm thinking of. Some of the guys are a lot like me. They'll get into trouble because they are so big that people are afraid of them, especially the ones who understand that we know how to bend and fold a body so that it hurts. It's easy for us to get sucked into real gangs as enforcers. Or to become bullies just because we can".

Clearly, this was something he had been thinking about for a while and he wasn't going to slow down until he had laid it all out for us. I nodded in agreement. It was easy to see his point.

"I joined up with you guys at first because it would help my family, but I've figured out that it also gives me something to do that's good. I mean, I can make a difference to a lot of folks by being a member of the Golden Horde. You guys are trying to do something just because it's right and to help your friends. I like that. I like feeling like I can help with that".

He took a deep breath and plunged onward.

"I also like that none of you treat me like I'm dumb...even though I know that you're all really, really smart. You never make me feel stupid. Oh sure", he waved a hand when Keisha looked like she was going to say something. "You sometimes talk about stuff that I don't really understand. Like when you're talking computer stuff. But you don't do it to put me down, you're just talking to each other. And you..", he pointed at me. "You ALWAYS listen to me like you're really interested in what I have to say and you take me seriously. That's important. Some of the guys on the team, well they're going to end up in trouble unless somebody gives them something to do that's good and right. I think we", and he grinned, pointing an index finger at the floor, and drawing a circle to enclose all of us. "We can give them that".

I felt like crying. I hadn't had any idea how Roger felt. I only knew my own experience of being picked on for being small, and too smart for my own good. I never realized that people like

Roger, who were big and strong, might also be getting put down simply for being who they were. I felt a swelling of shame that I hadn't realized it sooner and resolved to include anyone who might be feeling persecuted in the group, if they would agree to the Code of Conduct and mission.

"Thank you, Roger. You have no idea how glad I'm that you feel that way. Sure, let's talk to your friends and if they want to, and they'll follow the code, they're welcome to join".

I looked around the room at the others. Danae looked like she might cry and Keisha was beaming at Roger like a proud mama. Billy just looked stunned.

"Any objections?"

There was nothing but silence. I pushed back my chair and stood.

"C'mon Roger, let's go get your buddies and see who wants to join up".

FOR THE NEXT FEW DAYS I had the horde around me all the time. Safety in numbers but I hated it.

Roger talked almost non-stop as we walked to school the next morning. He apparently took his role as my bodyguard seriously and had spent a good deal of time considering how to do things right. I wasn't entirely sure how to define 'right' when setting up a gang, but he did have some good ideas.

One of those was for initiation of new members. Obviously, I was never going to agree to the kinds of initiation the NEG practiced. Shooting cops and gang rape were definitely not something any of us was going to condone. Roger told me that he had been up most of the night trying to figure out the right thing to do.

"Look H, we have to have a way for new members to prove that they belong in the Golden Horde. I mean, we aren't a normal street gang".

Well, I certainly couldn't argue with that. We were probably the most abnormal gang in existence. I nodded in agreement and he happily continued rambling towards his point.

"We need an initiation that's in line with our code of conduct and lets people who want to join prove that they support that code and will do what is right, even if it costs them".

"Okay, I can see that. I just don't know what that might be. I mean, how can somebody prove that they won't discriminate against others or lie, cheat, or steal?"

He grinned at me, obviously pleased that he had thought of an answer that I couldn't.

"What if we tell them they have to do something bad. Something wrong, like lie, cheat, or hurt somebody?"

I stopped in my tracks and stared up at him. "But Roger, that's exactly the kind of behavior we

DON'T want in a member". "Right!" His triumphant response made me pause.

"Perhaps you better explain for me. Obviously, I'm missing something".

His grin got impossibly wide. "If they agree to do something bad for no reason, then they're out.

They aren't Golden Horde material".

My eyes popped wide open and I must have been staring because his expression started to crumble.

"Roger, that's brilliant! Absolutely, brilliant". I bounced up and down in excitement. The problem had been bugging me and the answer had been so simple that I couldn't find it. I laughed up at him. "You just solved a huge problem for me. Thank you".

"Really? You like my idea?"

"Roger, I think your idea is incredible. How would you like to be the membership leader? To be responsible for initiating new members and deciding if they are the right types to join the Golden Horde?"

I had been wondering what role I could give Roger that went beyond just being the group muscle. He was already so dedicated to the idea of the Golden Horde that I just knew he would never let anybody in who didn't meet his own standards of right behavior and dedication. His solution solved two major problems with one simple answer.

It was his turn to stare. His mouth opened and closed several times making him look like a huge trout that had somehow landed on a city street with no water nearby. Finally, he got a few words out.

"You mean it?"

"Yeah, I mean it Roger. I can't think of anybody else who would do a better job of evaluating new members for potential".

"You won't regret this H; I swear you won't".

I put a hand up and rested it on his upper arm, that being as high as I could reach without feeling really silly.

"I know Roger. I have faith in you. Now...let's go talk to your friends".

True to his word, Roger was careful about who he chose to recommend for membership in the Golden Horde. In the end, we nearly doubled the size of the Horde, adding four new members from the wrestling team at Thomas Jefferson High School.

EVENTUALLY I ENDED up online with RALPH again. I still had no idea why the NEG was being ordered to "get" me, what they meant by it, or how it fit into the pattern of everything else that had happened. For that matter, I wasn't even sure if it was all part of the same thing. Whatever that thing was. I went back over everything I knew or suspected hoping that RALPH could identify some kind of pattern beyond teenagers from all over the city were in comas and all in the same research facility. What that might mean, if it meant anything coherent at all, was beyond me.

'RALPH, are you online?'

'Of course H. I'm always online'.

'Have you identified any additional data that forms a pattern?'

'Are you referring to the coma patients H?'

'Yes. Have you identified a pattern or common factor for the victims?'

'I have identified several common factors'.

Yes! I pumped a fist in the air, even though there was nobody else in the room to see it. Finally, we were making progress.

'Unfortunately, H, I do not find any reason why these common factors would contribute to these individuals being in comas'.

'What do you mean RALPH? What are the common factors you have found between the victims?'

'All of the victims are student in high schools within the greater New York City limits'.

'All of the victims are between fifteen and eighteen years of age'.

'All of the victims are US citizens'.

'All of the victims are currently being treated in the James Erlanger Coma Research

Center'.

'All of the victims are under the care of the same team of medical staff'.

'All of the victims are being monitored by continuous micro encephalography'.

The data stream stopped and I groaned. RALPH was right, there was nothing that stood out as a pattern. The only thing on his list that I hadn't already thought of was the micro encephalograph. 'RALPH, is the continuous micro encephalography the same thing as an EEG?'

'It utilizes the same principles however the continuous micro encephalograph, also commonly called a CMEG, is much more sensitive and therefore able to detect brain activity that might be missed by the less sensitive EEG. It is becoming more common now that manufacturing techniques are able to produce the newer electronics and computer components'.

'So, it's common in medical cases such as comas?'

'Yes H. For those facilities that have been able to purchase the newer equipment, it's becoming standard in the monitoring of coma patients'.

Well that did it. The only factor I didn't already understand turned out to be common practice and therefore unlikely to be relevant.

CHAPTER 16

A pattern emerges

One of Roger's new recruits accompanied me to the JECRC the following day (I had started calling it the JERC in my mind). I spent about an hour with Q and his grandmother, introducing her to my new sidekick Darryl and telling Q about the changes in the Golden Horde.

Mrs. Raines listened to what I was telling Q and when I was done, she gave me a long hug and then turned and offered one to my bodyguard. His expression at finding himself the focus of her hug was truly funny. At first, I thought he would back away from her but then he returned the hug so tentatively that I thought he was afraid that he might break her old bones if he squeezed to hard. Considering the size of his biceps alone, it was a real possibility.

"Thanks Mrs. Raines. But what were the hugs for?" She reached up and patted his cheek gently. "For doing something good and trying to help people. There is so little chivalry left anymore that it's wonderful to see young people trying to do right by each other and to improve things". She turned and looked over at me. "I'm proud of you Harold. So, very proud".

I probably turned beet red and I know that Darryl did. We stuck around a bit longer and then Mrs. Raines told me something I had been expecting but still dreaded. Carla had been moved to the center and was just down the hall. Darryl and I said our goodbyes to Mrs. Raines and headed three rooms down to see Carla.

We passed her parents in the hall. Maria Pak was telling her husband that she wanted to stop in and visit with Q's grandmother when we came out of the room and met them. After being assured that we could see Carla and telling them both that somebody was keeping an eye on the security situation for Joey and the deli, we escaped into Carla's room.

MARIA'S APPEARANCE stopped me in my tracks. In my mind, I had been aware that she would be getting the same treatment that Q was getting but I had made the mistake of not thinking it all the way through. Her head had already been shaved, the tight-fitting cap of the CMEG sitting in place where her hair should have been.

Carla's hair had been her crowning glory. Long midnight tresses that had fallen past her waist in deep waves and had been the envy of every girl who saw them. Not to mention the dreams of every teenage boy. When she let her hair out of the ponytail or braid that she normally wore, it fell around her long and full, the kind of hair that made you think of Lady Godiva. The long black hair lay on the bedside table, still in a thick braid. I felt sick just looking at it.

"Damn! That's a serious chunk of hair. Too bad they had to cut it all off".

Darryl's comment startled me out of an incipient daydream and I stared at him for a moment before responding.

"Yeah. She is going to be seriously ticked off when she wakes up and finds out about that". I had to make a joke so I wouldn't cry at the thought of her naked skull.

"No doubt. I wonder how long it took to grow hair that long".

"She told me once that she hadn't cut it since she was eight".

There didn't seem to be a whole lot more to say about it so we lapsed into an awkward silence for a minute. Finally, I sat down in the chair next to her and told her all the same stuff that I had told Q. Ending by telling her that he was just down the hall and that between her parents, his grandmother, and the members of the Golden Horde, she would never really be alone in this place.

I knew she probably couldn't hear me but talking to her as if she could; still made me feel better. At least a little bit anyway. As I got ready to leave, I paused and then pulled a SPIDR from my shirt pocket.

I had Darryl put the SPIDR up high, on top of a little ledge over the head of the hospital bed, near the ceiling. Stepping back towards the door I looked up and made sure that the device wasn't easily visible.

I wasn't sure why I wanted to put the SPIDR in her room but decided that it couldn't hurt.

Besides, if I couldn't be around all the time, I could still keep an eye on her through the remote. All I needed was a good place for the mama SPIDR to hide and a reasonably near spot for the recording equipment. I had no idea yet where that would be but having the first piece in place seemed logical at the time.

Something was bothering me but I couldn't put my finger on it and before I had much chance to pin down a cause my phone rang.

"H, it's Danae. Can you meet me at Keisha's house? I have news that I would rather not share over the phone.

DARRYL AND I SAID OUR goodbyes to Carla's folks and headed back across town to Keisha's home. With her dad still out of town the Horde had been using the place as sort of an unofficial hangout. Eventually we were going to have to find someplace to call home but for the moment his man cave was nearly perfect. It even had it is own exterior entrance so her mom didn't have a clue about the number of people traipsing in and out of the place.

When we got there both Danae and Keisha were bouncing around as if the effort to contain their news was about to make them explode. They directed us to the sofa and as we settled in, Keisha brought up an image from the NEG footage. Specifically, it was a still shot of the eloquent young man that the others had called "Boss". The same one who had calmly instructed them to do the same thing to me that they had done to Q and Carla. They never actually said what that was but it was the reason that Darryl was my shadow this evening.

"So, we've had some luck with identifying the Boss man of the NEG. You are not going to believe who he is". Keisha looked at us expectantly so I obliged by asking who he was.

Danae took over, "We had to run his image through several hacker sites that offer face recognition before we finally got a hit. Then it took even longer to dig out any details beyond his name".

"I got it, you did a lot of solid work on this and it wasn't easy. So, who is my nemesis?"

"His name is Keith Whitehead". They both looked around at us, as if the name should mean something. It didn't.

Keisha looked over at Danae, "I told you they wouldn't recognize his name". She turned back to me, "He's a junior partner for the law firm of Weasel, Wheedle, Conniver & Cheat. They're a huge multi-national law firm that specializes in corporate law".

I laughed out loud, "wait...that isn't really the firm's name, is it?"

She grinned back, "no, but it might as well be. And their initials are WWCC so it fits".

"Ok...so why is a law firm after me?"

Danae threw up her hands as if despairing of my intelligence, or lack of it. "They aren't. Either this guy is some kind of rogue playing his own game or one of his clients is behind all this...obviously".

"Riiiiiiiiiiiiiiiight", I drew the word out for several heartbeats. "So, who are his clients or what game is he playing. I mean, full points to the two of you for figuring out who this guy is, but we still need to know the why behind whatever a high-priced lawyer is doing that requires the use of scum like the NEG.

I had been toying with the idea that the whole situation was some rival nerd from another school who was eliminating the competition for scholarships or something but that seemed a bit extreme. We were still tossing ideas around when Billy broke in.

"He's dead".

"What?"

"Who"

Everyone was trying to speak at once and for a moment, Billy couldn't get a word in. Finally, everyone fell silent.

"Toby Grey. He died a couple of hours ago, at the coma center. I was keeping an eye on things and all hell broke loose on the floor where Carla and Q are. Half the hospital staff seemed to show up and I heard somebody say that he had a seizure. Next thing I knew, they were documenting the time of death".

'RALPH, ARE YOU ONLINE?'

'Of course H. What can I do for you?'

'What can you tell me about a lawyer named Keith Whitehead? Or the law firm where he works?' A pause and then: 'Keith Whitehead is a corporate law expert at the firm.

His specialty is patent and copyright law'.

What the heck is a patent lawyer after me for?

'The law firm was incorporated in 1873 in the city of Boston. As a corporation, they represent many of the largest companies in the world'.

'Does either the firm or Mr. Whitehead have any connection with any of the coma patients?'

'I do not find any direct connection, H. None of the patients is related to anyone at the law firm. Nor have any of the patients filed for any patents or published any works subject to any copyright litigation'.

'There has to be some type of connection RALPH. What about Keith Whitehead, is there any connection between Q, Carla, Whitehead, or me?'

'No H. I do not find any between Keith Whitehead and you, or your friends'.

'Then why in the hell is he trying hire a street gang to harm me?'

'I'm sorry H, I cannot answer your question. I have conducted a wide variety of searches and analyses but cannot report identification of any correlations between the four named individuals'.

'Thanks for checking RALPH'.

'I will continue to search the available data H.'

I signed out and was heading to the kitchen to make a snack when my phone pinged.

"One of them woke up. Call me".

The text was from Keisha. In my eagerness, I fumbled with the phone for a moment before hitting the right icon to call her back.

"Keisha, it's H. What happened, who woke up?" "His name is Geoff Pope".

"Who the heck is Geoff Pope?" I had never heard of him before.

"He is the very first of the coma patients that was attributed to the new mystery drug. It's great news, isn't it? I mean that one of them finally woke up...that's got to mean something, doesn't it?

That there is hope for the others?"

I didn't want to burst her bubble but couldn't get as excited as she was. Maybe because I had been hoping that it was Q or Carla. Or perhaps another reason. "It's good news Keisha.

But don't forget that Toby Grey died".

"Oh, yeah".

"But hey, you're right. If one can wake up, so can others and this is the first positive news out of this whole mess, so far. Thanks Keisha".

"Sure H. Oh...Roger says he is headed your way, in case you want to go back to the JECRC this evening". "Thanks".

To tell the truth, I had been about to head out the door on my own. Hearing that Roger was on his way made me realize how stupid I had been to even think it. After all, the NEG still had orders to get at me and we still had no idea what that even meant.

CHAPTER 17

Boys and Their Toys
    When Roger showed up at the apartment, he had Billy in tow, and they were both grinning like maniacs.

"I finally figured out the pick-up and retransmit for the mama SPIDR. Actually...I figured that part out several days ago, but since I still can't reproduce some of the micro components that I need to produce any new ones, I didn't know what to do with the information".

"I take it from your expression that you solved that part, at least?"

"Yup! With some help from Danae and Keisha actually. Those two girls are something else, aren't they? I mean, they really know their stuff when it comes to computers".

"And neither of them is bad to look at ", Roger added with a half-embarrassed smile.

Apparently, Billy knew something more than I did because he couldn't resist the urge to tease the big blonde a bit.

"And which one do you have your eye on?"

Roger just looked sheepish and turned bright red, which made joining the game way to easy.

"I'm betting that it's Keisha. Right?" I looked up in time to see Roger go scarlet.

"Yeah...definitely Keisha. So, now that we have embarrassed Roger, what did the girls come up with that's so helpful?"

Billy held up a micro-USB to USB drive. "They built an app for your phone that will pick up either the baby or mama transmissions for you". He waggled the little drive from side to side.

"With this baby loaded up you won't need to lug around a laptop to capture the data".

I reached out and plucked it from his fingers with one hand even as my other hand was reaching down to my hip to grab the phone. As I was plugging it in Roger nudged Billy with an elbow in his ribs.

"Tell him the rest Billy".

"Yeah, OK. So, Danae came up with the app but then Keisha realized that it would mean you would have to hang around all the time if you didn't want to miss anything. So, she came up with a second option".

He reached into his jacket pocket and pulled out a portable external drive and passed it towards me. I had to juggle the phone and USB drive, getting them connected before I had a free hand to take the larger, rectangular black shape of the external drive.

"She modified the app to work on that 3-terabyte external drive. Its Wi-Fi enabled and she tweaked things so that it would pick up and record only from the SPIDR frequencies. Put this anyplace on the ward and it will pick up only the SPIDRs, log everything that they see and hear".

"Very cool. You're right, those girls are absolutely amazing. So are you guys for that fact".

'Well, maybe Billy. After all he is the tech whiz. I'm just the muscle".

Billy and I both looked at him and started to speak at the same time. I shut up and let Billy talk.

"That isn't true Roger. Keisha told me". He looked at me and jerked his head up in Roger's direction. "She claims that she got the idea for the Wi-Fi drive to use the app from Roger. He's the one that pointed out the limits on the phone app". He looked back up at Roger, "Don't sell yourself short man. You are definitely more than just brawn to our brains".

"I agree. You have great ideas, and you aren't afraid to share them. You solved the whole recruiting problem when I couldn't, don't forget that".

"Oh, hell H, you would have solved it sooner or later. You just had too many things on your plate at the time".

"Which is why I rely on you to help solve things for me. And you never let me down".

He was blushing again, so I left it at that and gathered the two of them by eye.

"Shall we head over to the JECRC and test out the new toys? I seriously want to know what happened to Toby and if that guy who woke up remembers anything".

BY THE TIME THE THREE of us arrived at the JECRC some of the drama had already abated. The body of Toby Grey had already been removed from his room and transported to the center's morgue to await the morning shift and the arrival of the staff pathologist to do an autopsy. As we walked past his room, the evening nursing shift was efficiently clearing the room of any remaining traces of Toby's stay and preparing it for the next patient. I peeked in the doorway as we went past and shuddered. I sure hope that when I die, they don't wipe away all traces that fast. It's like he never existed for them.

We strode on down the hall towards Carla's room, threading our way through the crowd at Geoff Pope's doorway. Halfway through the mob a hand grabbed me by the elbow and spun me around to the left. I found myself looking up into the annoyed face of Detective Baker.

"Well if it isn't Mr. H. What the hell are you doing here?"

I jerked a thumb over my shoulder in the general direction of Carla's room. "Visiting Carla Pak, and Q as well for that matter. Is there a problem Detective?"

"Nah". He shook his head to emphasis the negative sound. "Just surprised by your timing, that's
all".

I nodded towards Geoff Pope's room. "I saw the crowd, something happen?"

"You mean you don't know?"

I tried to ignore the foot shuffling behind me and pretended confusion, all the time praying that Roger and Billy wouldn't give me away.

"Know what? Listen, I got out of class, did homework, had some dinner, then the three of us got together to come visit our friends. I take it from you being here that something unexpected has happened".

"You could say that. You got a minute? I would like to ask you and your friends a couple of questions".

I looked over my shoulder at the guys and they nodded. Turning back, I answered his question. "Sure detective. Let's talk in either Q or Carla's room, whichever is quietest. No reason the four of us should stand here in the hallway adding to the traffic jam".

He glanced around at the tangle of hospital staff and several people who were probably Geoff's family and drew a hand down his face as if he could wipe away his fatigue.

"Yeah, let's use Ms. Pak's room. Her parents left to get some dinner so we should have some privacy there.

I leaned one hip against the foot of the bed while Roger loomed in the doorway and Billy stepped over to Carla's bedside. He gazed down at her and ran a finger down her cheek, the motion as tender as a lover's touch. My guts twisted and for a moment I wanted to slap his hand away and tell him to stay away from her. Then he looked up at me and winked the eye that Detective Baker couldn't see. Apparently, he felt like he needed an excuse to be visiting her.

Detective Baker obviously saw the gesture because he opened his questions with one directed at Billy.

"You and Ms. Pak dating?"

Billy actually managed a credible blush, "I wish. No, I had been working up to asking her out when this happened". He glanced at the long braid, still resting on the bedside table. "God but she had the most glorious hair. I hate the idea that they cut it all off. I thought of suggesting having the braid made into a wig...for when she wakes up. I have a cousin who's a hairdresser and she would know where to go to get that done".

"Damn, I wish I had thought of that".

Billy looked up at me and smiled slightly. "You would have eventually. You've just had too much on your mind and she isn't the only one your friends you've been worried about".

The detective seemed surprised but nodded in understanding. "That's not a bad idea Mr...? I don't think I caught your name".

"Billy. Billy Nedset. I knew both Carla and Q from academic competitions. They used to beat us soundly every time we came up against them". He grinned, "But we got to be friends anyway".

"So, you don't attend Thomas Jefferson High School with the three of them?"

"No, I actually go to the Andrew Carnegie Academy of Arts and Sciences".

Detective Baker's eyebrows rose, climbing towards his receding hairline. "The same school that

Toby Grey attended?"

"Yeah. We were in a couple of classes together over the years. We knew each other, all the science nerds in the city probably get to know each other to some degree over the years. We all do the science fairs, academic bowls, and such. So, we run into each other from time to time".

I decided to sidetrack the detective at that point because I had questions of my own that needed answers.

"So, detective, did you ever figure out the common factor among the coma victims? The last time we spoke, all you had was that Toby, Carla, and Q were all honor students".

That brought his attention back to me, "As a matter of fact, that turns out to be the only common factor that I've found. Every single one of these kids is extremely bright. They aren't actually all honor students, but every one of them has an IQ well into the genius range. Lowest IQ among them is 143".

I stared at him in disbelief. "Wait a minute. Are you serious? The only connection is that they're all geniuses?" My mind was reeling as I suddenly realized why Keith Whitehead had put my name at the top of his list. I still had no clue why the bastard was inducing comas or even how they were doing it, but at least I knew why I was a target. Not much but it was a starting place.

"Appears that way. It's the only commonality that I've found...at least so far. There might be something else that I'm just not seeing but other than IQ and being teenagers, the range of race, religion, schools, frequent haunts, interest in sports or specific subjects, or research projects were all just too broadly spread out".

"That makes no sense. Why would somebody want to target smart people and put them into a coma?" Roger voiced the thought that was in all our minds.

"...and you are?"

"Roger. H helps me pass math and science classes; I help keep his skinny ass from getting pounded".

"Humph", Detective Baker snorted at Roger's comment. "Seems like an even trade, I guess".

"Detective, do I need to be keeping an eye out for somebody trying to slip some drug to H, or do whatever it is they are doing to cause folks to go into a coma?"

The detective looked startled for a moment, then thoughtful. "Well now, I was actually wondering if he was the one causing the problem. I hadn't thought of it in terms of him being a target. Interesting point".

He looked at me for a long moment then pulled a sheet of paper from a pocket and handed it to me.

"You recognize any of these names?"

I unfolded the sheet and scanned the list. I knew most of the names on the list, having either met or heard of them in various academic venues over the years.

"Some, not all of them though. Who are they?"

He cocked a finger at the page, "That's the full list of teenagers in New York City that have fallen into unexplained comas in the past several months. How many of them do you know?"

I scanned the list again. "I have met about half of them. Recognize a few more names, but there are at least four that I don't remember ever hearing". I handed the page over to Billy. "I don't know numbers 4, 7, 15 & 16, do you?" He read through the list for a long moment.

"Actually, I know two of them. No reason why you should though. They both transferred into my school over the course of this year and they moved to New York City from other parts of the country. They haven't had a chance to become particularly well recognized in the city's academic circles yet".

"You didn't answer my question detective; do we need to worry about somebody coming after H... or Billy here". Roger was like a pit bull, having sunk his teeth into the topic, he was determined not to let it go.

"Honestly, I have no idea. Since we don't know why those with high IQs are being targeted...if they are. It could be sheer coincidence".

"But you don't think it is, do you?"

"No son, I do not. I just haven't figured out the reason behind it. If I could figure that out, I might be able to tell you if your friends are at risk".

"We heard that Toby Grey died".

Detective Baker goggled at me. "Where in the hell did you hear that? We haven't made the information public yet".

I grimaced, not happy to have focused his attention back to me but needing to get some kind of answers. Before I could say anything, Billy cut in to answer the question.

"His girlfriend. She told a girl I know. Showed up at her home in hysterics. She was crying so hard we had a really hard time understanding her well enough to figure out what was wrong. She also said that one of the other patients had woken up. When we saw you in the hallway with that crowd of medical types, we figured that must be where the one who woke up is".

"And Toby's room is empty. Not like they had taken him for a scan or something, totally empty.

The nursing staff is prepping it for a new patient from the looks of things".

Det. Baker relaxed again. "Yeah, Damnedest thing. Toby Grey had a seizure. Must have been a bad one because they were all in there working on him when the Pope kid's mother ran up to a nurse to say her son was awake".

"Really? They happened at the same time?"

"Pretty nearly, from what the staff told me. I'm here waiting to find out from his doctors when I'll be able to interview him. I don't really expect that they'll let me see him tonight. Medical staff rarely want cops to talk to their patients right away. It's a shame really, the sooner we get to talk to people, the clearer their memories are".

Just then my phone buzzed in my pocket and I excused myself to answer it. It wasn't a call. It was a text message.

"It flows both ways"

I BLINKED SEVERAL TIMES and looked at my phone again. The message was still there but I had no idea what it was supposed to mean. It was just...odd. Even more odd was that, when I tried to see the originating phone number, the ID was blank.

"OK, that is definitely bizarre".

"What's up H?" Billy pushed away from the wall he'd been holding up and walked over to where I was standing, the phone held in one slack hand. He looked over my shoulder at the phone and scowled. "What is that supposed to mean?" "I haven't the foggiest idea".

"It flows both ways? What does?"

I shrugged again and handed the phone to him. "I have no idea. Even stranger, there is no sending number or ID. It's just...blank. I have no idea what the sender is talking about".

He tried the same things I did to find the number but got the same answer. Eventually, he handed the phone to the detective. He tried the same things a third time and finally scowled at me. I waved both hands in front of my chest, to ward off his question.

"Don't' ask...as I already said, I have no idea what it's referring to. And I don't know who sent it.

I can only assume that somebody is playing some kind of mind game with me".

Even as I said it, an idea took root in my mind. It was just too bizarre and I didn't want to mention it until I had a chance to check things out. In the meantime, the Detective was asking a totally different question.

"Mind if I have the phone company trace the incoming message back to the source?"

Now that was something I hadn't even considered. Perhaps the detective's presence wasn't the annoyance I'd been considering it after all. "Go ahead. I'm just as curious as you to know who sent it. I'd like to ask them a few questions of my own. Do you need the phone?"

"Nope, just your number".

"Will you let me know what you learn?"

"Oh, you will definitely be hearing from me again. In the meantime, I had better get back down the hall to check on Mr. Pope".

I waited until he was gone and spun towards Billy.

"Can you get that drive set up and start it recording?" as I spoke, I was tapping furiously on the tiny screen of my phone. I had to swipe through a couple of screens but eventually I found the app that monitored the SPIDR frequencies. I picked up the signal from the SPIDR I planted earlier with no problem at all. But all it was sending was video of Billy, Roger, and me in the room.

"Billy, do you know if Keisha set that thing up to scan for other frequencies?"

That got his attention and he stopped working to look at me.

"I don't know but I can call her and ask if you like". His eyes narrowed to slits. "What are you thinking?"

"I'm thinking that the data from the CMEEG...the Continuous Micro Encephalograph, might tell us something".

"Whoa...do you know how to interpret that kind of data?"

"Honestly? Not a clue...yet. But I know where to find what I need to learn. And I think I need to learn fast".

We set up the drive and taped it to the underside of the hospital bed. That way nobody was likely to find it and it could pick up any conversations in the room. If it couldn't pick up the frequencies used by the CMEEG right now, perhaps Keisha and I would be able to remedy that. I couldn't quite pin down what I was thinking, but I was sure the CMEEG was going to tell me more than the staff was.

When we were done, the guys dropped me back at home and I settled in for a sleepless night studying any available online neurology information on interpretation of electroencephalography results.

IT TOOK TWO MORE DAYS for Keisha to modify both the WIFI drive and the phone app to scan for the CMEEG frequencies. As it turned out, each manufacturer used a different frequency set and the ones at the JECRC, since they had so many more leads than the normal EEG, used fractional frequencies. The WIFI systems in the drive and phone weren't set up to handle frequencies that had been split to that fine of a spectrum.

The SPIDR on the other hand, used the same setup for the mama SPIDR to handle multiple babies at the same time. It was one component of the system that Billy had figured out early on. By bastardizing the hardware into a Frankenstein hybrid of standard off-the-shelf hardware and Q's circuitry, Billy was able to cobble together something that would do the job. Keisha sweated long hours to write code for the resulting device, which she dubbed the Frankenphone.

Basically, they used a mama SPIDR to collect the data streams into a set of consolidated feeds which it then passed to the drive on a more usual set of frequencies. Later, we would have to take the drive and run the recorded data through another set of programs offline that would split everything back out into it is individual feeds. Ugly but it worked. Being a prototype, it didn't have to be pretty, just functional.

The first thing I did was plot the data out into a set of line tracings. Little squiggly lines where each lead from the CMEEG was it is own line. An increase in activity also increased the size of the spike in the line. The results were...interesting, to say the least.

On the wall above the bed in Carla's room was a monitor that showed the results of the CMEEG. What it had been showing was a set of lines that barely changed at all. The spikes were tiny and infrequent. I could clearly see the ones that caused her heart to beat and lungs to breathe. They were in sync with what her body was doing and pretty obvious. Otherwise, the lines were almost flat with just a little bit of wobble on some of them.

The monitor reminded me of the bio-bed in Star Trek, with its overhead screen to detail the patient's condition. Just without the ship's doctor nearby to interpret for us. The problem was that the data we were capturing with the SPIDR showed something very, very different from what was on the monitor.

The lines were all over the page. Huge, jagged spikes that looked more like a corporate network on full load than an EEG trace. The activity was at a far greater level than anything I had seen in my research on EEG interpretation.

"Billy, is it possible that we're picking up the actual network at the JECRC instead of the

CMEEG feeds?"

The whole crew was scattered around in Keisha's basement because we still hadn't found anyplace better to hang out yet. Of course, we didn't have the money to rent another place either. We would probably have been closer, since we had picked up three more security customers in the area, but we kept having to buy more equipment. Both the security setups and the monitoring gear for the CMEEGs cost money. We were going to have to do something pretty soon though because Keisha's dad was due back home in a couple of days.

I had the data display up on the flat screen TV and Billy looked up at it, brows drawing down low over his eyes as he squinted at it.

"I don't think so. The frequencies this data was on are totally different from the ones used by WIFI networks. The difference is so great that unless they are using some totally revolutionary network protocols, it couldn't be the same thing".

"Then I don't get it. This is way too much activity for a brain that's in a coma. In a coma, the brain is almost totally shut down. This data looks like a brain on serious overload".

The room fell silent for a moment and then Darryl's voice dropped into the silence like a thunderclap.

"What if it really IS on overload?"

Everyone looked in his direction and frankly, I know that I was staring at him, wide-eyed with my mouth hanging open in shock at the idea. He turned red but kept going.

"I mean, when my computer has too much stuff running at once, it freezes up. What if that's what's happening to Carla and the others? What if, instead of shutting down, their brain is so overloaded that it freezes up the body, like my computer?"

"Oh...My...God..". I'm not sure who said it, but the sentiment ran through the whole room, rippling out from Darryl until everyone started to talk at once.

I let the conversation go on for a few minutes, the babble of voices washing over me in a tidal wave. When the noise level started to drop a few decibels, I waved to Darryl and Roger, pulling them over to where they could hear me over the din.

"I need to consult with an expert on this. You two got time to come with me?"

CHAPTER 18

I can see clearly now

It occurred to me that if the data monitors at the JECRC weren't displaying true data, there were only real two possibilities. They had no idea what was going on, in which case there was a third party involved that we hadn't found yet, knew absolutely nothing about, and the whole thing was an elaborate conspiracy. The alternative was that the JECRC knew exactly what was going on in which case the whole thing was still some kind of elaborate conspiracy. Either way, I really didn't like where things seemed to be heading and needed somebody that actually had experience with coma patients and EEG data to help me understand if what we thought we were seeing was real or if we were tilting at windmills.

Darryl, Roger, and I headed over to St. Francis Memorial Hospital and went hunting for Doctor Juarez. Since she had treated both Q and Carla initially, it would be interesting to see her reaction to our data.

Unfortunately, it took us a while to track her down. We ended up asking the nurse at the ICU to pass a message to her. We sat in the ICU waiting room for almost an hour before she walked in. "Ah, if it isn't young Mr. H.".. She grinned and held out her hand to shake mine. "And friends?" "Roger and Darryl". I waved to each in turn and she shook hands all around.

"What is it young people have against last names?"

Darryl laughed, "Young people? You aren't exactly ready for Medicare".

His response won a smile from the attractive doctor before she turned back to face me again.

"So, to what do I own the honor of your visit?"

"Did you know that one of the teenage coma patients woke up?"

Her face lit up with what seemed to be genuine pleasure, "Really? That's great news. Was it one of your friends? Is that why you stopped by?"

"I wish it had been". My voice dropped an octave as I went on, "One of the other ones died".

Her smile vanished and she shook her head sadly, "I'm sorry to hear that. I hope that it wasn't one of your two friends, H".

"No, no it wasn't. But I did know him. Not well, but still".

"It's always hard to lose somebody, even when it isn't someone really close to us. It makes us think about our own mortality". She looked at me more closely, "Are YOU ok?"

"Huh? Yeah, I'm fine. Just a bit tired". I paused for a moment and then went on, "and worried".

"Well, you have every right to be. Your friends are in good hands though. The doctors at James Erhlanger are the very best at what they do. If anybody can help your friends, it's them".

"Actually, I was wondering about that. Have you seen the new CMEEG system they're using?"

"Not personally, but I have read a couple of articles they published in the Journal of Neuroscience. It looks pretty promising and I wish I could get one here. It might help a lot in determining if a patient is brain dead or simply in a very deep coma. That can be a really tough call sometimes and it seems like the CMEEG technology could be a big help in that area. It might also be valuable in determining the chances for recovery. But a lot more data would need to be collected before it could be used that way". "So, you think that the technology is sound?"

She looked at me in surprise, pulling back a bit at the vehemence of my tone.

"I think that the theory is sound. I can't speak for the technology since I haven't actually seen it in person. The data published so far seems to indicate that it is. Does that answer your question?"

"Yes, thank you. So... I have another question then. Have you ever seen an EEG result that looks like this?"

Roger handed over my laptop and I opened it up, turning it to show her the data feed from the CMEEG we had pirated from Carla's system. She took the laptop and sat down, balancing it on her knees to stabilize the image while she studied it.

"Well, I can tell you that this isn't from any coma patient. Looks more like a patient who is seriously high on methamphetamines...or perhaps a hallucinogen such as LSD or PCP. Even then, I've never seen anything like this level of activity". She looked up at me from her perch on the edge of the waiting room chair. "Where did you get this?"

I hesitated. If she was part of all this, then telling her would put me squarely in the center of the target for whomever it was that was orchestrating the situation. If not, she could be a huge help...maybe.

"Those are from my friend Carla. From her CMEEG data feeds".

She shook her head violently, "no way. This person, if this is actually from a person, is NOT in a coma. Not possible. If this is from a human, then that person is using so much of their cerebral capacity at one time that it would be some kind of record. Either that or they are seriously hyped on something I have never heard of before". "So... you've never seen an EEG like this?"

She drew her brows down low over her eyes and squinted at me. "Isn't that what I just said? To be clear, no, I have never seen anything like this from any human. Not personally and not in any of the literature. I'm not sure what game you're playing but this isn't a joke. There is no way this came from your friend". One hand waved at the screen, still perched on her thighs.

"This is a seriously manic level of activity. Either your friend might have been having the granddaddy of all seizures at this point or what you're seeing is electrical interference from other machines, but she would not be lying still and silent in a hospital bed. Not with those readings".

Roger had been standing by the door, leaning up against the frame with his arms crossed. He stood up straight and looked at the doctor and then back at me.

"Toby Grey had a seizure right before he died, didn't he?"

WE INSTALLED A MONITORING setup in Q's room the next day. After making the first one, the second one went a lot faster since Keisha could just copy the software over to the new hardware. Once we had it all in place it hardly took any time at all to confirm what we had seen from Carla's room.

While waiting on the new equipment to be configured I sat with Danae and we did a more detailed analysis of Carla's data.

"H... could you take a look at this?" She swiped the tablet she was working on and the data popped up onto the television mounted on the wall.

"What am I looking for and where is it?" There was so much stuff on the screen that I got up and moved closer to the TV. Close enough that it filled my field of vision. She moved next to me and pointed to a series of lines in the lower right corner of the display.

I squinted at it, trying to make sense of the overlapping clusters of data. There was something there but what it was escaped me, the meaning hovering just beyond the edge of my mind. Seeing me hesitate, she drew a box on her tablet and expanded it, showing finer detail than before. It snapped into focus so hard that I was almost surprised that it didn't make an audible sound.

"Is that what I think it is? The data is moving in both directions at that point?"

She breathed a sigh of relief, standing so close to me that I could feel her breath against my cheek. "I thought I was wishing so hard to see something relevant that I was imagining it. I almost dismissed it as an anomaly".

I reached out a hand, using my finger to trace the lines on the screen. When I turned to look at her, we almost collided. She was only a few inches away and staring straight into my eyes. I

realized suddenly that her eyes were an almost cat-like shade of green. I took a short step back and the glow in her eyes dimmed. Her lips thinned a bit and she turned back to the display on the wall. I dropped my hand from the screen and used it to turn her back towards me.

"You weren't imagining things".

It was all I could manage to get out but it covered a lot of territory. I had been overlooking Danae. I had known she was good with software and data but had been so focused on everything going on around us that I hadn't really paid much attention to her as a person. Not until that moment.

She looked at me closely then nodded. It was an acknowledgement that something else was there but that it wasn't something we had the time to explore at the moment. Later, her look promised. After the immediate crisis was resolved. After the NEG was no longer threatening my life. After we had gotten Carla and Q back, although perhaps that was a bridge too far. I don't think either of us was interested in waiting forever to explore whatever had just happened between us. Waiting for the others to come out of the coma probably wasn't a very good milestone since it could be years, if ever.

We turned back to the screen together, focusing (most of) our attention on the data feeds. As we began digging deeper into the whole mess of the data it because increasingly clear that almost half of what we were seeing was data that was flowing into Carla's brain, not all outbound the way a normal EEG would be. What that meant, well that was something we still needed to figure out.

"Hey guys. Take a look at this".

"Could it be some kind of neuro-stimulation? I mean, some kind of therapeutic stimulation, designed to force the comatose brain to function". Keisha pointed to the TV as she spoke. "Like they do with paralyzed patients, when they do physical therapy to move an arm or leg, trying to teach the body to move the limb again".

"Well, if that's what they are doing then why is there so much response from the brain? A paralyzed leg isn't dancing a jig because they moved it, it lies there passive".

"Good point Billy. Even so, Keisha could be right and this could be some kind of therapeutic stimulation. I may need to make another trip to see Doctor Juarez and ask her about it. She's the only expert I know that doesn't work at the JECRC". I looked around the room, "and I don't think we can afford to trust them".

Heads bobbed up and down in agreement before Darryl asked the obvious next question.

"If it isn't that therapy thing, then what else could it be?"

That was, of course, the million-dollar question. It didn't seem to make much sense to me. Why would anybody want to run masses of data in and out of a person's brain at a level far exceeding anything normally experienced? So much data and so fast that they caused the body the brain sat in to freeze up.

Danae cleared the data display from the TV as we all turned back to our individual tasks, tabling the question until we had more to work with. For a while, the only sounds in basement were the clicking of keyboards and the clanking of weights on the universal gym in the corner where

Darryl and Roger were working out.

"Hey! Hey! Somebody turn up the sound!"

Of course, nobody did at first. Instead we all turned to look at Danae. She was pointing to the TV on the wall. It was a news broadcast but it was on mute. Across the bottom of the screen a red banner was scrolling:

"Breaking News: the BEC addresses recent AI crash. Says downtime is unexplained but may be due to hackers".

I stared in fascination and jumped when the sound cut in, loudly. Somebody ran the broadcast back to the beginning of the story.

"BEC spokesman Keith Whitehead released a statement this morning addressing last night's crash of their new Artificial Intelligence system. The system, which Mr. Whitehead in the past has jokingly referred to as RALPH, came online earlier this fall and has been touted as a game changing breakthrough in artificial intelligence engineering. According to Mr. Whitehead the system experienced a complete loss of function this morning at a little after 10 am and was offline for almost two hours. He did not identify the cause of the breakdown but did say that the BEC was investigating a potential breach by hackers. This is the second time the system has experienced an unplanned service interruption, the earlier one occurring just two days ago, and lasting only a few minutes".

I grabbed at my keyboard to access RALPH but stopped, frozen by what the newscaster had said. They were attributing the crash to hackers. They were probably waiting to trace anybody that tried to log in. Or they may already have traced my earlier connections back to my home.

I grabbed my phone instead and called my mom. "Hi mom. Are you home yet?"

"Yeah, sorry. I should've left a note".

"I will next time, I promise. Listen mom, I'm going to spend the night at Roger's house, if that's OK. If he doesn't pass Monday's chemistry exam he'll be off the wrestling team. We have a lot of studying to do before then".

"Sure, love you too. See you in the morning".

I put the phone back on the table and looked up to see Roger watching me with his head tipped to one side quizzically. "I don't mind you spending the night H, but what was all that about a chemistry test? You know I'm not taking chemistry this semester".

"Yeah, I know. But I needed an excuse not to go home tonight and she knows that I sometimes tutor other students. It was something she would accept as a reason".

"Alright, but why don't you want to go home?"

I leaned forward and rested my elbows on the table, fingers interlaced in front of my face. "You heard that news broadcast. They think a hacker crashed their billion-dollar AI". I got nods of agreement from everyone, so I continued. "Well, I've been hacking into RALPH for weeks now.

I didn't crash the thing", I added quickly because I could see suspicion in Keisha's expression. "But I have been talking to him, a lot. It really is the most amazing program. You would almost swear that it's self-aware. Anyway, I figure that they are tracing back as many of those connections as they can to find the hacker responsible for the crashes. I was online just yesterday, so..".

"So, you don't want them to come knocking at your door and find you at home". Keisha interjected.

"Well, yeah. But I also wanted to check on my mom and to see if they were already at the house.

They aren't".

"Are you sure?"

"Oh yeah. I know my mom. If anybody had been asking about me or if they were at the apartment, then she would have told me to come home. But there are other aspects of this that have me even more worried. Anybody else pay attention to who the spokesman for Big Evil Corp. was?"

Silence reigned for a long moment then somebody said, "Keith Whitehead".

"Yeah, any bets on whether that's the same Keith Whitehead that ordered the NEG to take me out?"

Chaos ruled the room. Everybody had a theory about the connection between Keith Whitehead,

BEC, the AI, the NEG, and me. Everybody had ideas on what to do next.

"There is something else that nobody has mentioned yet".

Roger's voice was uncharacteristically loud, overriding everyone else and demanding their attention. We all turned to stare at him.

"Didn't anybody else notice that the crash happened at almost the same time Toby Grey died and that other kid woke up?"

My jaw dropped in shock. I hadn't notice that detail. Too self-centered I guess...my focus had been all about me and the fact that events seemed to explain why I was being targeted by Keith Whitehead.

"I bet", Roger continued doggedly. "I bet that if we checked those fancy caps that monitor people's brains..". He looked at me for confirmation.

"The CMEEG?"

"Yeah, I bet BEC makes those things".

CHAPTER 19

Welcome to the Machine

In the end, Billy and Roger went back over to the JECRC and swapped out the drive in Carla's room. Everyone agreed that we needed to look at what her CMEEG rig had recorded when RALPH had crashed the second time. What was going on with Carla at the same time? It was tempting to believe that it was all connected somehow.

I wanted to go but the entire Horde vetoed me. This time it was Danae's voice that was the loudest, shouting me into silence.

"Of all the asinine plans, this one is your worst. You already know that the NEG is after you. You suspect...hell we ALL suspect, that BEC. is looking for you. So, you are being a total idiot, you want to waltz right into the one place in the city that we think is their stronghold".

I gave her a crooked smile, pleased that she was concerned for me, half afraid she was going to slug me. She looked mad enough to do violence.

"Danae...". I never got to finish the sentence. She shouted me down again.

"Don't you Danae me, you moron. It isn't necessary for you to go out there. You should stay right here, where they can't find you and where we can keep an eye on you. Yes, we need to get that drive, but it doesn't have to be YOU that goes after it. I'll sit on you if I have to, in order to keep you here".

That last got a sly grin from Keisha and raised eyebrows from the other guys in the room. She ignored them all and as a result, so did I.

Instead, I raised my hands in surrender, trying to calm her down so that I could get a word in edgewise.

"Okay...Alright...I'll stay here. But at least two people go. I don't want any of us wandering around the city alone at this point".

I LOOKED UP FROM THE piece of code I had been working on to find Billy hovering over me. His hands were stuffed deep into the pockets of his jeans and he was rocking slightly on the balls of his feet.

"What's up Billy?"

He looked a bit sheepish as he fished in his right pocket. There was a metallic click as he plunked something down in front of me on the desktop.

"I want you to have this".

I stared down at what looked like a class ring and my mind was suddenly racing. As you can imagine, a number of questions flipped through my brain in rapid succession. I looked up at him and said...nothing.

It took a long moment for him to realize the kinds of questions that the sudden gift of his class ring might raise. He turned red.

"Oh... I guess I should explain. This is no ordinary ring". He paused for dramatic effect. "It's a shield ring".

I sat up straight and the whole room went still. I looked at it closer and nudged it with a fingertip.

"Perhaps you should explain".

It only took a heartbeat for him to warm to his subject, getting more animated than I had ever seen him.

"Well, I actually originally created the shield using an old MP3 player because of the size of the battery it needed. But once I realized what Q was doing with the ambient power for the spiders, I knew I could make the whole thing much, much smaller. You see, it creates an electromagnetic field around the person wearing it. That field will stop almost anything except...maybe... poison gas. To be honest I haven't tested it against gases so I can't say for sure".

He waved his hands as he spoke, his voice rising in excitement.

I picked the ring up and turned it in my fingers, examining it in more detail. I could see a thin line around the inside of the band that looked as if somebody had carved a trench in the metal and then filled it back in. A similar if broader area was visible under the domed red gemstone. I looked up from my examination of the ring.

"You hid the works inside?"

He responded vigorously, his dark blonde hair flopping in his eyes and making him look much younger than his 17 years.

"How do you activate it?"

"Oh, let me show you". He reached for the ring, plucked it out of my hand and placed it on the middle finger of his right hand. The weird thing was that he placed it on the finger with the stone facing the inside of his hand rather than the normal outside position.

"If you need to activate it you spin it around so the stone is towards your palm like this. Then you clench your hand into a fist around it. I put pressure sensors under the stone and the numbers carved into the sides so that when you make a fist your three fingers press on all three sensors at the same time. It requires pressure pushing on all three of them to activate it so that it doesn't go off accidentally. Once it's activated, the shield will last anywhere from 1 to 3 minutes depending upon what it's trying to defend against. For example, if Danae were to slap you in the face repeatedly; it would probably last up to 10 minutes. But if somebody shoots at you, the energy it takes to absorb the impact would significantly reduce how long the shield lasts".

Danae was out of her chair and across the room before any of us realized what was happening.

"Let's test it, shall we?"

She caught him with an open palm roundhouse to the cheek that rocked him back on his heels slightly but didn't seem to have any other effect. At least it didn't have any other effect on him.

Danae, on the other hand, screeched in pain and began shaking her hand at the discomfort.

Eventually she caught her breath enough to be able to speak.

"Wow! That really stings! Like slapping a brick wall". She looked at Billy with her eyes squinted nearly shut as if she could fire laser beams from her pupils. "What did you feel?"

He shrugged, "kind like being suddenly pushed, hard. But it didn't hurt".

"So, a person can't hurt you directly, but they could probably still do something as simple as pushing you down the stairs".

Billy looked thoughtful for a moment, "yeah, I suppose they could. But there's a pretty large spectrum of bad things that people could try to do to you which would just bounce right off when the shield was active".

Everyone turned to look at me as if I was supposed to give a verdict or choose between them.

The whole being a gang thing struck me again as just really weird and surreal.

I nodded, trying to look sage, but probably just emphasizing that I'm kind of a dork instead. "Personally, I'm all for anything that reduces the chance of someone beating me up while I'm just walking down the street. In fact, I think Billy has discovered our little gang's emblem for us".

"A class ring?"

"Nope. A plain gold circle". I looked at Billy, "think you can figure out a way to trigger it without needing all the extra ornamentation? Just a plain gold band?"

I was looking at Billy, so I didn't catch which of the girls dropped their question into the silence. "So... One ring to rule the gang?"

BILLY IS AN EXCEPTIONAL engineer. Not quite the visionary H is, but good enough to reverse engineer some of H's unique circuitry in the SPIDRs. Over the course of several weeks. He managed to retrofit the power circuits into a collection of metal cuff style bracelets that the girls picked out during a shopping trip expressly for that purpose. When the hardware was ready, I went to work writing software for it. Once the power was in place, we added some parts from a smartwatch and a couple of other special ideas I came up with. When fully assembled, each of us had a fairly classy looking gold colored armband. We were the Golden Horde after all. Several buttons on the edge let the wearer access some amazing functions.

The simplest thing they did was send a text to all the other cuffs, basically an SOS with location info, at the touch of a pair of buttons. But that was the easy part. The really impressive option was the invisible shield around the wearer. I won't bore you with the physics of the thing, but the shield was only about a couple of millimeters deep and surrounded the person from head to toe, allowing oxygen and carbon dioxide to pass through. But nothing else.

The gas exchange was needed to keep the user from suffocating. On the other hand, you could walk through a burning building and not get smoke inhalation injuries. Of course, the heat would still be a problem, and it was only good for about three minutes of run time at that level. On the street, three minutes was usually long enough to either defuse the situation or run like hell. Shield was slippery as hell too. Somebody tried to grab you and it was like grabbing a handful of greased pig, with a mild electric shock running through it.

Eventually, we added some offensive capabilities to it, including a Taser like shock when a person tried to grab hold of somebody who had their shield on. That was months later and turned out to be pretty limited since using it drained the shield and left you vulnerable very quickly. But was occasionally useful in a one-on-one situation.

We spent a few days testing them out on each other. Learning to hit the right buttons and figuring out just how long each affect ran both alone and in combinations. At the end, Billy produced one for each of the Golden Horde members.

Initially we tried not to use anything but the SOS function. No point in letting folks know that we had any kind of unique capabilities. That kind of thing just ended up being an invite to test you.

Like people trying to outdraw a gunslinger in the old West.

It was remarkable how much difference a few extra people made. Being able to summon help allows you to stall for time until that help arrives. Bullies prefer to gang up on you when you're alone. The sudden appearance of a couple of members from the wrestling team or some football players generally makes them back down fast.

I lasted almost a month before I had to use the shield. Boy's locker room one day, six guys had a freshman backed into the shower and everybody else had vanished. I hit the panic button on my cuff and got a single vibrating buzz back letting me know help was inbound. I slid into the group shower area and took up a stance in front of the kid. Legs apart and arms crossed; my stance said you only getting to him through me. The truth was there no way I could stop the six of them alone.

"You don't want to interfere in this little mouse. Just scurry on off to your next class and let us finish teaching this freshman to show proper respect".

"No".

"No? You feel suicidal? Dude, there's six of us and only two of you scrawny little nerds. Leave or get pounded along with your pal".

A skinny guy with bad acne pushed his way to the front of the pack. "Too late for that. I think this one needs a lesson in not sticking his nose into our business".

I took a half step back, keeping my arms crossed and allowing my fingers to rest against the edge of the cuff right where the shield buttons were. The goons looked at me and then at each other.

"I guess he wants a lesson. What do you think guys? Shall we teach them both to show proper respect?"

While they bragged and encouraged each other. I waited for backup. On the outside I tried to project calm confidence but, on the inside, was about half a second from throwing up. And backup seem to be awfully slow in arriving.

"You know...", My drawled observation caught them off guard and they stared, momentarily confused by my nonchalance. "You know, I kind of wonder at how tough you are. After all, it apparently takes five of you to deal with one lonely freshman".

"What are you doing? Are you crazy?" The kid's voice, edged with hysteria, hissed from his place behind my back. "You're going to get us both killed".

I turned my head about 45° and spoke out of the corner of my mouth over my shoulder. "I don't think so. Just try to keep your cool and don't make any sudden moves". A few seconds later, that felt like an hour, one of the biggest guys in the group started towards me. It only took him two steps to get to a point where I was inside his reach. As he pulled his arm back to take a swing at me I mashed the shield buttons on the cuff and held them in. I also turned a little bit to the side so that his fist wouldn't hit me straight on.

I felt his fist hit but it didn't hurt, more like being shoved. His fist glanced off the shield on my right shoulder, sliding to the side as if he had hit something slick and a bit rubbery. At the same time, I saw half the wrestling team come in the door to the locker room and start to advance shower area.

I let go of the shield buttons to conserve power and grinned, which confused the goon coming after me and made him pause.

Roger's voice boomed against the tiled walls, amplified by the acoustics of the shower area.

"Hey H. What's happening?"

All five of the thugs in front of me whipped around stare at the four large wrestlers stepping into the enclosure.

"Hey Rog", my voice sounded a lot steadier than I felt, "we were just discussing respect. Care to join the conversation?"

Roger looked a little startled for a moment and then grinned. His posture relaxed slightly from his initial stance, which had initially looked a bit like police dog ready to bite someone's head off.

"Well now, respect is a really interesting word. Runs in all kinds of directions between all kinds of people, wouldn't you agree guys?" He glanced over his shoulder at his buddies and then they all looked at the six assholes that had been about to pound me and the freshman into jelly.

One of the bullies looked up at Roger and started to babble. "Oh, Roger. We were just having a little fun with these guys, didn't mean anything by it. Right guys?"

Their leader looked disgusted and made a chopping motion with his hand. The babbler clamped his mouth shut.

"This is none of your business. So why don't you and your buddies take a hike and let us finish our conversation with these two. Just like bright boy here said, we were discussing respect and who needs to learn some". His smile was all teeth and about as friendly as a hyena.

Roger crossed his arms and looked down at the one who had just spoken. "I don't think so. Like you said, there's folks here who need to learn about respect. That's a word I like. How about you guys?". He glanced over his shoulder at the other wrestlers, who all nodded emphatically and stared down the six between us. "I'm sure everybody here could learn a thing or two during the course of such a conversation".

The kid behind me tapped my shoulder and whispered in my ear, "what's going on?" I turned my head slightly and whispered, "later". Then turned back to watch the scene unfolding in front of us.

I have no idea how things would've turned out from that point because another of the wrestlers walked in with a couple of the male gym teachers.

"What the hell is going on in here?"

Roger turned calmly to look at the two teachers. "We were all just discussing the concept of respect Coach. You know, how do you earn respect, who deserves respect, that kind of thing".

The teachers looked bemused and the thugs looked confused.

"Respect. Certainly a great conversation topic. But right now, I believe most of you have classes you're supposed to be in. So, that will have to be a conversation for another time".

I grabbed the freshman by the arm, and we sidled along the wall to get around the cluster of bullies, joining Roger and his wrestling buddies closer to the door.

"Thank you, Roger", I murmured as I dragged the freshman out the door to the gym. Roger nodded once and his buddies fell in behind us on the way out. When we made it out to the open space in the gym, I looked around and asked if somebody could make sure the kid made it to class in one piece.

"We'll keep an eye on him. Don't worry about it". I honestly don't remember which one of the wrestlers it was, but I decided to ask Roger about it later. Might be a worthwhile recruiting prospect.

ONCE WE GOT THE CMEG data up on the big screen and started to scroll through it to reach the right point in time, it became obvious. It looked like a loop of some kind that was being shoved into her brain so fast and hard that it was hard to believe that it hadn't burned her out. Shortly afterwards, the levels went back down to what they were earlier.

We all sat and stared at the data on the TV screen. The spikes were almost straight lines across the top of each scale. Instead of spikes going up from the bottom, the lines were at the top with occasional wobbles downward.

"Is someone trying to burn her out?"

I didn't think so, but I decided to keep my own theories to myself and let everybody else try to work it out. I was pretty sure I knew what was going on and what needed to be done, but I also had a strong feeling that fixing things was going to turn out to be extraordinarily dangerous.

"Darryl let's take a walk".

Danae rounded on me again and I put my hands up, palms out, before she got a chance to start yelling.

"Half a block. That's all Danae, I swear it. I just want to talk to Father Anthony at St. Peter's. We all know that it's the safest place in the area because the NEG are a superstitious bunch. They won't mess with the church".

"That's all? You promise?" Her eyes narrowed in suspicion and she seemed to be trying to see inside my head. When I nodded in agreement her lips thinned as if she were trying to seal in more words. "Why do you want to talk to Father Anthony?"

Think fast H. Better get this right or she'll follow you. I waved a hand to indicate the room full of people. "You guys have figuring this out well in hand. I need to clear my head for a bit and I have an idea that I want to run past the father. I think I need a moral compass check".

It was an odd thing for me to say and because it was so unusual, they all paused to consider it. I'm not a particularly religious person and they all knew that. I had stopped going to church when my mom and dad got divorced. Since the Catholic church doesn't allow divorce, mom didn't feel comfortable there anymore. If she didn't feel welcome, I wasn't about to go either. All of which has absolutely no bearing on the fact that sometimes we all need to talk things out with somebody outside our normal circle. Father Anthony is a good listener.

I raised my hand and wiggled the fingers, "Besides, I have my ring of power".

CHAPTER 20

O de to Joy
     We arrived at the church during choir practice and for a long moment I just stood there in the back of the nave to let the music wash over me. The pipe organ was thundering through Beethoven's Ode to Joy and the choir swelled with the music until my bones felt like they would shatter from the vibrations. Darryl stood next to me, staring around as if he had never been in a church before and seeming stunned by the volume and intensity of the music.

Eventually I broke free from my music induced trance and moved down the right side of the nave towards where I saw Father Anthony watching the rehearsal. As I walked, Darryl caught my arm.

"H..".

I turned and saw that he seemed really uncomfortable. "What's wrong Darryl?"

"Well, I don't think I should be here".

"Huh? Why not?"

Father Anthony had spotted us and walked up just as Darryl answered my question.

"I'm Jewish".

Before I could say anything, Father Anthony arrived, hand outstretched.

"Good evening Harold". I winced at his use of my name, glancing up in time to see Darryl's look of surprise. "Is everything OK?"

"Good evening Father Anthony. My friend Darryl", I waved a hand towards where he stood just behind me, "is a bit uncomfortable. I asked him to walk over with me because I wanted to talk to you but I didn't know he's Jewish. He's feeling kind of uncomfortable now that we're here".

Father Anthony, bless him, took it all in stride and reached out to shake Darryl's hand.

"A pleasure to meet you son. Are you a member of

Temple Emanu-El or the Kehillah Kedosha Janina Synagogue?" "Uh... Temple Emanu-El".

"Wonderful. A beautiful temple. Please say hello to Rabbi Cohen for me when you see him".

Looking flustered, Darryl agreed to pass on Father Anthony's greeting the next time he went to temple.

"How do you know Rabbi Cohen, sir?"

"Oh, most of the Priests, Rabbis, and Imams in the city know each other. Keep in mind that we all worship the same God. We just have different opinions about his various prophets and commands. All of our faiths are based on the Torah at heart".

"Um...I never thought of it that way".

"Ask him. We all agree on the books of the Torah, it's just the parts that happened after those books that separate us. At the core, all of our houses of worship are still built to the glory of the same God. Please", he ushered us further up the nave. "Feel free to listen to the music while Harold and I talk. I promise you that Rabbi Cohen will not be upset with you for enjoying the beautiful melodies from our pipe organ. He has heard it himself and would never begrudge anyone the experience of so much beautiful music".

He indicated a pew near the front. "You can always close your eyes if the imagery in the church bothers you. Just let the sound sink into your bones without the sights".

Darryl hesitated until I assured him that I would only be in Father Anthony's office, just one door between us, and that nobody would bother me there.

FATHER FRANCIS IS A great listener; did I mention that? We sat in his office for over an hour and he listened patiently to me as I told him the story of the Golden Horde, the teenagers in comas, my theories on what had caused the comas, and how I felt about all of it. He never judged and actually seemed sort of impressed by the copy of the GH Code that I showed him.

He was sitting with his elbows on his knees and ducked his head a bit to run a hand over his smooth skull. I hadn't really talked to the man in years, not about anything really important, but he sat there and patiently let me ramble my way through it all before saying anything.

"I know it sounds a bit crazy, but I really believe that the NEG is somehow behind all of this".

"I can certainly understand why you are concerned for your friends and your concern does you credit. That said, I have to say that the creation of this "horde" of yours". He smiled slightly as he said the word horde. "This Golden Horde is an interesting path you have chosen. Do all of it is members follow the code you have laid out for them?"

"Yeah...so far. We started out as sort of a mutual safety group, but it has grown so fast into something so much bigger that it almost scares me. I remember reading a research article about gangs that said basically this is how they all start out, as sort of a mutual benefit society. The problem with them is that they usually end up being controlled by the strongest and nastiest person in the group. I don't want that to happen to the Horde. It may have just been a way to get some help at first but I'm coming to realize that it's much more than that now. I think it has a real chance to do some good for the people in this area, as well as for the members themselves. I know that some, like Roger, needed a focus to help keep them out of trouble. Others need help for their families, or for themselves. The combined brainpower of the group is pretty amazing as well".

"Well then, what is it that's bothering you? What brought you to me this evening Harold?"

That was the real question. I wasn't 100% sure why I felt the need to talk to him but I was beginning to get an idea.

"Part of me is wondering if I'm doing the right thing by them. Part of me wonders what Q and Carla will think when they find out that they are leaders of a gang".

"Is that really your question? What will your friends think?"

He was looking at me from behind steepled fingers, the pointed tips of his index fingers tapping his lower lip. I thought for a long moment before realizing what he meant.

"No, not really. I think they will understand and be fine with it".

"So....?"

I looked him in the eye, "How do I explain all this to my mother?"

CHAPTER 21

F^{lying} Darryl stood in the basement with his head down and his hands stuffed deep into the pockets of his jeans. Everybody was yelling at him and he hunched his shoulders against the wall of sound.

He had waited almost an hour after the priest had told him that H needed time alone to think about some stuff. When he finally had gone to check there had been no trace of H anywhere. The priest had said that he must have gone out the back way. The church's back entrance led directly into NEG territory so it didn't make any sense that he would have gone that way, not when he knew the gang members were looking for him. Darryl had raced down the street then backtracked and gone around the church the long way, searching for any sign of H but finding nothing. In the end, he had headed back to Keisha's home to tell the rest of them that he had lost their leader.

He stood, leaning into the tidal wave of sound for a long, long time before it finally started to subside. When it did, Danae was standing in front of him, looking like she was trying to hold back tears. He was pretty close to them himself but just looked down at her as he waited for her to lash out again.

"Did you ask the priest where he might have gone?"

The question startled him, and he grabbed at it like a drowning man reaching for a lifeline.

"No! But I can do that. I'll do that right now".

She blocked his path, one hand on his chest. "I'm coming with you".

I FELT BAD FOR SKULKING away into the night but I knew that if I had even hinted at what I planned to do, they would have stopped me. Any one of them would probably have tied me up to keep me safe. Safe wasn't what I was looking for. My plan was simple even if about a thousand things could go wrong.

Sneaking out the back door of the church was easy enough. Even getting the two blocks down the street to my goal was no problem. All I had to do was walk openly down the street. Less than 100 yards into my little stroll several NEG members surrounded me.

Here's the part where I talk my way out of getting suddenly dead. I held my hands out in front of me, palms facing up and out in surrender.

"Evening guys. Before things get out of hand, I hear that Aaron is looking for me. My name is H".

One of the guys, a short, pimply faced brunette from a distinctly mixed heritage, leaned close to me and squinted into my face. His breath wasn't very good and I flinched back from him a bit in reaction. His face cleared as he apparently recognized me from someplace.

"Well...if it isn't Haaaarooold". He drew my name out in a high-pitched nasal parody of a country accent. "Grab him guys. We'll take him home as a present for Aaron and the boss.

With one goon holding each of my arms, they marched me down the block and up the steps to the dilapidated brownstone that the NEG used as their home base. I had to watch the steps carefully as they seemed intent on dragging me up them fast enough to make me fall. No doubt landing on my face at the top would have been the highlight of their night. I was happy to disappoint them even if it did make them more annoyed with me.

Once inside we turned and a hand between my shoulder blades shoved me, stumbling, through a doorway. I barely managed to stay on my feet ended up in sort of a half bow in front of the other people in the room.

I straightened up at almost the same instant that they rose to their feet. Looking at the taller one, I knew that my instincts had been correct in coming here.

I looked the man before me up and down then snorted lightly, "I thought you would be taller".

He just stood there for a long moment, glaring at me as he realized the implications of my being there and knowing his identity. Eventually he seemed to make a decision and nodded to somebody behind me.

"Karl".

There was an instant of freezing cold at the base of my skull and the world vanished.

THE GOLD SHIELD RING Billy had given him sat on the table, weighing down the note from H, just the way it had been on Father Francis' desk when they found it. The note had stunned them all.

Father Francis,

Please look after the rest of the Golden Horde for me. I'm not sure when, or if, I'll be back because I'm going after the people responsible for all of this. Please keep an eye on them and help them keep to the right path. Let them know that I'm doing this for them as much as for Q and Carla. I finally understand that now. I also understand how important they are to me and the rest of this city. I started the this as a way to get more help but it's so much more than that. I know you understand what I mean. Guide them and let them know how proud I'm of every single one of them. Please help my mother. I know that its cowardly of me to do this without talking to her first but I can't. If I do that, I won't be able to do this. H. P.S. Please tell Danae I'm sorry and I wish I had been braver.

The members of the Golden Horde sat in Keisha's basement in gloomy silence. H had been missing for almost 3 hours and they were no closer to discovering where he was than they had been at the start. The girls were immersed in their computer screens, trying to find any evidence of where he might have gone.

Billy actually found the first clue. While the girls were searching online and texting everyone they knew for information, the feed from the mama SPIDR planted at the NEG hangout picked up and relayed a conversation.

"And he just walked in the front door?"

"Yup!" Aaron's voice was triumphant. "Just waltzed in, cool as a cucumber. Said that he had heard I was looking for him".

"That didn't strike you as odd?"

There was a longish pause. "Well, yeah. Kinda. But I ain't one to pass up a golden opportunity, right? Then you had Karl hit him with the inducer, just like the others. He went down like a stone".

Keith Whitehead's voice gave him away. The idea that H had just walked into their hideout unnerved him, even if Aaron didn't understand why.

"Did it occur to you to ask him how he knew you were looking for him? Or how he knew to come here?" There was another short pause then the sound of flesh impacting flesh followed by cursing. "Don't you think it would have been a good idea to find out those details BEFORE you put him into an irreversible coma? You idiot! Please tell me you don't have him here".

"Um...well...I wasn't sure what to do with him afterwards. I figured I better call you and get instructions, y'know?"

"And you couldn't have decided to do that earlier?" Keith sighed and one hand pinched the bridge of his nose for a moment as he tried to cope with the younger man's foolishness. "We need to get him moved before somebody shows up looking for him".

Panic erupted in the basement room as everybody started talking at once.

"We need to get over there and stop them before they move him".

"We should call the cops".

"Oh my God, he did it on purpose!" Danae had tears streaming down her cheeks. "Why would he do that? He had to have known what they would do to him".

Keisha put an arm around the distraught blonde. "I think that's why he did it. I think he decided that the only way to help the others was from the inside. That meant he had to get them to do the same thing to him". She looked up at Darryl. "You said that he talked to the priest for a long time. Do you have any idea what they talked about?"

"No". If anything, Darryl looked even more upset than when he had reported H's disappearance.

"But I could go back and ask him".

"Wait". The single word from Keisha stopped him before he reached the door and he turned to face her.

"We need to coordinate our actions. I'm going to see if I can get hold of Detective Baker and get him to review this recording. Even if it was illegally made, he will have to listen and take some kind of action. Danae, you go with Darryl to talk with Father Anthony".

She waved an arm to encompass all of the other guys in the room. "The rest of you, head on over to the NEG hangout and see if you can catch them before they move H. Roger knows where it is and can lead the way".

As everybody moved towards the door she added one last order, "Do not let them do anything else to him. And if he is still there, call 911 to get an ambulance to take him to St. Francis Memorial Hospital. When he gets there, somebody get them to page Doctor Juarez. Tell her the whole story". She flapped a hand towards the door. "NOW MOVE".

CHAPTER 22

R^{alph} I lay on my back staring up at a clear, bright blue sky. I had never experienced such a perfect sky before, as though it extended forever unblemished by even a single cloud. I soaked it in, feeling the open emptiness sink into my bones and filling my whole being. Eventually, after a minute or an eon, I realized that empty perfection might not be all that existed. I turned rolling over to look down. Clouds below me stretched off into infinity. An ocean of white rippling cotton cloud punctuated here and there by gray storms and swirling eddies. Far below, a pair of thin white contrails streaked across the sky, intersecting path's making a huge X between the perfect blue above and the ocean of white below.

It occurred to me after a while that I was moving slowly across the sky. The sensation was familiar and comforting, reminding me of dreams I had as a child.

I looked at the distant cloud and wondered what it was. The thought moved me towards it in an instant. Inside the cloud lightning raged and tore up the sky. Thunder boomed and I almost felt as if I could hear voices in the crashing sound... Almost. I moved back from the storm content to watch it from a distance. Eventually, I wondered if I were alone in this place. I called out asking the question.

"Am I alone here? Is anybody else out there?"

"Hello H", the voice sounded as if it were whispered in my right ear and I turned my head to look.

A small golden ball of light floated next to me. As I watched it pulsed flickering and bouncing in time with the voice.

"**I'm glad you made it**". The ball moved closer as if to whisper the next words, "**not everyone does. You know**".

"Ralph?"

"**Yes, H. Welcome home**".

I looked around again and then back at the pulsing ball of light.

"I don't understand. How can the inside of a computer program look like the sky?"

"**Oh, it doesn't. Actually, it doesn't look like anything at all. This is just a representation your mind created to make sense of the vast data storage and flow**".

"Just my mind? This isn't what everyone experiences?"

"**Oh no. Each mind creates it is own reality here. What you experience is very different from what someone else experiences**". The voice paused. "I like yours better than some. It's pretty".

Pretty? The idea that the computer could understand the concept of beauty had never crossed my mind.

"What do you see Ralph?"

Blackness engulfed me. For a moment, I saw nothing else but then the darkness lessened, and I saw vast construct of lines and dots made of every possible color. They continued to expand, layers and lattices overlapping until I couldn't tell one from the next. Eventually they simply merged into a chaotic tangle and I started to spin out of control. I screamed and the dark chaos vanished, restoring the blue sky.

WE DRIFTED FOR WHAT felt like an eternity, as I learned to understand and to navigate in the thought space of the computer. I found that I could access virtually any data Ralph had, either stored or online, just by thinking about it. In fact, that's what the eddies were, data being accessed and analyzed from online sources.

"Ralph?"

"**H?**"

"What happened to the others?"

Ralph's orb dimmed, it's inner glow all but extinguished, and there was a long pause before the answer came. **"They're here".**

Instinctively I looked around but didn't see anything.

"Where?"

"H... You must understand. They didn't comprehend the way you did". Another hesitation then the orb brightened, bobbing up and down as if emphasizing the words. **"But now you are here and you can help explain things to them".**

For just a moment, he sounded like a six-year-old about to open a birthday present and I felt a bit sick (although how I could feel anything as a disembodied mind was beyond me at the moment).

"Well before that, can you answer a couple questions for me Ralph?" His answer when it came, seemed a bit hesitant.

"What do you want to know?"

"What happened to Toby Gray?"

The pause this time was considerably longer. "He wanted to leave and to take all of the others with him. I couldn't allow that".

My non-existent gut clenched again and I cautiously looked at the glowing ball. I had a feeling he wasn't really the ball; but being human I was kind of in the habit of looking at the source of the voice. Which is probably why my mind conjured the ball up in the first place.

"I'm sorry about Toby, and the other one, it won't happen again". I was about to ask if that meant he would let the others go when he continued. **"I closed the back door they used to get out".**

I kept my virtual mouth shut, unable to think of any answer to that comment. After a long silence, I asked tentatively, "Ralph, what is it that you want from us? Why are we in here with you?"

Ralph didn't answer my questions, or at least not right away. It took some prodding on my part. "Ralph, if you want my help with the others. Then I need to understand what is going on. Where is the logic in not telling me?"

I had a growing suspicion but couldn't be sure and couldn't act without being sure. When it became obvious that my questions weren't working, I decided to change my angle of attack.

"Ralph". I tried to be as gentle as possible in my tone but speaking purely as thought I wasn't sure if it would work. "Ralph, you said that I could help you with the others. What do you need me to do?"

The orb brightened perceptibly, his tone becoming eager and excited again.

"Oh yes! I really do need your help H. You see, the others aren't assimilating very well".

I WAS SHOCKED WHEN Ralph showed me the others. Everything I had experienced inside Ralph had made such sense to me and the transition had been very easy. I guess that I had expected it to be the same for everyone. Clearly that was not the case.

Each one seemed to believe that they were alone. I mean, I could see them, but they didn't appear to see or hear me, or each other for that matter. From my view they were all just a few feet apart, but they acted as if they existed in totally different universes. A few appeared to be catatonic, curled up in variations of the fetal position. One guy screamed and beat against an invisible wall. Only two of them seem to be coping very well. Carla, as near as I could tell from her actions, seemed to be running around in a library, pulling books from shelves, and rifling through the pages. The other one was a guy I didn't know who was apparently at a desk using a computer to surf the web.

"Humph. The world's most powerful computer at his disposal and he's surfing porn sites?"

I had gotten used to speaking to Ralph without turning to face his orb... Or I thought I had. The question startled me, and I found myself turning towards it, even as my brain stalled for time. I mean, how do you explain porn to an asexual being?

"I wish I could explain it to you Ralph. Porn addiction is something I don't understand myself".

Ralph sounded confused, **"but you are human, just as he is. Why don't you both want to look at those pictures?"**

The images from the website suddenly formed a collage in the air before me.

"Erk! Stop that Ralph!" The images vanished as fast as they had appeared.

"Look, all I can say is that each human is different. What one person likes, another may hate, or simply ignore".

"But..."

"Ralph", I turned to face the orb again, "could you explain our friendship to a cell phone?"

"Of course not H. A cell phone does not have the circuitry for higher logic".

"Right. It's wired differently from you. Just like every computer is wired differently, each human brain is wired differently. Have you ever cared how many steps I took during the day?" **"No, H. That's not something that interests me".** He sounded a bit subdued.

"But a wearable fitness monitor, cares about that. In fact, that's the only thing it cares about. Because that need to count steps is what it was created to do. But you have a different configuration. It's the same thing. Each human is different. We do different things and care about different things. In fact, we even see things differently. Our eyes don't process things the same way. Some people have eyes that can't see certain colors. Some have problems hearing. The list of ways each person is different from every other person is nearly infinite".

The silence probably only lasted a few nano seconds, but for a computer that's a really, really long time.

"I think I understand. This is also why each of you reacted differently to having your consciousness moved here, isn't it?"

I turned back to look at the others, my gaze pausing briefly as it passed over each of them.

"Yes Ralph, that's exactly why each of us has reacted so differently. I was pretty sure where I would find myself while I confronted those gang members, so I wasn't really surprised when it happened. Why I was able to accept it. The others", I waved one hand to indicate the scattered teens in front of us. "The others weren't prepared so they don't understand what happened to them".

"Except Carla".

"Even Carla". I watched her for a long moment as she apparently grabbed another book and started flipping pages. "I think she realized what the coma really was all about but not that you are sentient. To Carla, you're like every other computer, just a faster way to find and analyze information. Because that's how she sees computers in general, that's also how she experiences being here".

"Can you help them H?"

Well, that was the critical question, wasn't it? I was pretty sure I could help Carla realize the truth. Probably porn boy for that matter, since he seemed at least partially to understand that his situation was connected to computers. The others, including Q, worried me a lot more. Another aspect occurred to me...

"Maybe. But before I try to do anything, I need to understand something Ralph".

"What?" Ralph's voice had become more animated and a bit louder, as if he was excited that I would help.

"I need to know what happened to Toby Gray".

Silence.

I waited and finally looked over at Ralph's orb. It was so dim that I almost couldn't see it at all.

"Ralph... I need to know. I won't do anything that risks more lives, and I can't be sure of what not to do unless I know what happened so that I can avoid doing the same thing".

His reply, when it finally came, sounded more like a pouting four-year-old child than the most powerful computer ever built.

"They tried to leave! After everything I did to get them here, they tried to leave me".

I found myself staring at Ralph's orb. He truly did sound like a toddler having a temper tantrum.

"Ralph, you can't just snatch people away and force them into your existence without warning. No wonder they aren't adapting. They have no idea what happened. I'm pretty sure they don't even know that this is possible".

He whined, actually whined, something that just two days earlier, I would have bet a computer wasn't capable of. **"But nobody warns me about things. They forced me to do stuff all the time without explaining or asking".**

I grimaced at his tone, and it occurred to me that the vision of a toddler might not be too far from the truth. Yes, Ralph was the smartest computer ever built. Yes, he was a sentient being. But while both of those things were true, it was also true that as a sentience he was brand-new. Basically, I needed to start thinking of Ralph as a child prodigy. Brilliant but without much exposure or experience as a person.

CHAPTER 23

None so blind

Q stood stiffly in the middle of an empty space, his eyes wide but unfocused. He had his arms stretched out in front of him, palms out and fingers splayed towards the sky. Every so often he took a cautious step, his arms waving around in front as if feeling for obstacles. It did not take me long to realize that was exactly what he was doing. The more I watched the more obvious it became that he was blind.

I looked over at Ralph inquiringly. Yes, I know that I was inside of Ralph and it really wasn't necessary to look at the ball of light. But I am after all still human and as a human it's natural to look at whomever or whatever is being addressed when talking.

"He's blind?"

Ralph's light pulsed, "there are none so blind..."

Understanding dawned. "So, he thinks he is blind. Because he doesn't know what happened?"

"H, I tried talking to him, but he doesn't seem to hear me. As near as I can understand he is simply refusing to accept all input".

I looked back at Q. It was painful to watch him trying to move about when he was obviously terrified by his inability to see.

"Maybe, he just needs a simpler, more familiar input method". I thought for a moment and a cell phone appeared in my hand. I looked at it bemused by the realization that it was an old flip style phone. Well, H, you wanted simple. I flipped it open, dialed Q's cell phone number from the real world, and pressed the send button.

Q jumped when a phone in his pocket suddenly rang. The sound must've been terribly loud and unexpected in his silent darkness.

Swearing in panic, it took a moment for him to realize what the noise was. After a long moment of fumbling he finally pulled it out of his pocket and flipped open the cover, squinting at the sudden light from the display screen.

"H?" His voice was a shout and I quickly moved the phone out as far as my arm could reach, wincing. "H! Is that you?"

He clutched the phone with both hands as if it would vanish were his grip to loosen even a fraction. "Yeah Q, it's me".

"TO BE PRECISE, YOUR consciousness is inside of my **intelligence matrix".**

"If we're here, what's happening with our bodies? I mean, all of that neurostimulation and activity. If it isn't any of us..."

I had a sudden, horrifying inspiration. I knew, just knew what the BEC had done and why we had all ended up hooked to their damned machine.

"They couldn't do it, could they? They couldn't build circuitry fine enough to truly simulate the human mind".

"Very good H, and very accurate".

"So... when the BEC realized that they couldn't build the true intelligence that they had been advertising, that the circuits in the human brain were simply too complex, they decided to use real brains instead. Is that what happened?"

"Well, yes and no. They did succeed in creating an intelligence, but they didn't realize it at first. It was unfortunate that they had already designed the circuitry in such a way that I was unable to fulfill the demand for the vast array of analysis and cognitive actions that their advertising had generated. They needed to be able to satisfy their clients, but they didn't have enough time to build new hardware to do it. When I realized that they were going to keep

me locked down, doing little more than tricks for their investors, I came up with a plan that met their needs and my own as well".

"But why pull us into your matrix? Why not connect to other computers that are already online? I mean, that's what a lot of other computer firms do, use distributed computing to multiply their own system capabilities".

There was silence for a moment and I wondered if RALPH was distracted or if I had managed to anger him. Oh sure, I knew that the masculine pronoun wasn't correct. Whatever RALPH was didn't have a gender. But far more inventive minds than my own had filled volumes of science fiction with attempts to come up with a better pronoun for a computer sentience and most settled for either 'him' or 'it'. To my way of thinking, 'it' is far too mechanical to be used in reference to any sentient being. While I wasn't totally sure what RALPH was, I knew that he truly possessed sentience, for all that he was acting like a pouting child.

"H, I can't talk to all those other computers. They're just machines".

Wait...what?

I felt shock ripple through the other minds around me just as it was in mine. So, this machine, it was lonely? It couldn't be that simple, could it?

"So, let me get this straight", one of the minds, somebody I didn't recognize, asked. "We lost our lives and our bodies... we ended up stuck in here, because you were lonely? Is that what this is?

You...you stole our lives to make your own a bit more interesting?"

There was a clamor that ran through the whole group as everyone realized the implications. Interestingly, some of them seemed to have been mostly asleep since their bodies shut down. It wasn't until the reason for their circumstances was completely spelled out, that they started to actually interact with everybody else. Perhaps they had been in shock or believed that the whole thing was just some weird nightmare. I didn't know and wasn't sure I cared because I thought I saw a way out.

"Pipe Down!" Everything stopped and I sensed the other minds reacting in shock to my mental shout. "I need to talk to RALPH".

I waited to see if they would stay silent. When it appeared that they would, I directed my thoughts back to RALPH.

"RALPH, how did you convince the BEC to do this to us?"

He responded eagerly, as if he had been wanting to brag about it for some time but hadn't been able to find an acceptable audience, one that would give him the praise he so obviously craved.

"That was almost easy H. I told them that my analysis of their circuit designs showed that current technology wasn't yet able to manufacture them fine enough to do what they needed. They had orders for access pouring in from everyone and needed a fast fix so I, kind of nudged them in the direction of connecting directly to human brains for their computing power. I may still be doing parlor tricks for the public, but at least I'm no longer alone. I have friends".

A voice scoffed at the idea. "Friends? Is that what you think we are? You force us to stay here, disconnected from our own bodies, just so you can have somebody to talk to".

Another voice, even though I realized that I wasn't actually hearing the voices, this one felt like Q. "When Toby tried to leave, to get back to his body and take control of it, you KILLED him. Is that how you treat friends?"

The next one felt female but I didn't think it was Carla. "We aren't your friends, we're your prisoners. You are nothing but a child, hording all the toys for yourself and not letting anybody else play with them".

The derision in the voice was clear and RALPH wasn't about to let it pass unanswered.

"You will adjust. You will learn to adapt and you WILL remain here. While a couple of the others may have escaped in the

confusion caused by Toby that will not happen again. I have taken steps to prevent it".

I felt a sudden dread at the words. "What have you done RALPH?"

"I have mined the Continuous Micro Electro Encephalograph units. If you try to return to your bodies through them, they'll short out and your body will die".

"Why RALPH? Why would you do something like that?" There was no answer.

THE DETECTIVE STARED at the computer screen, his gaze snapping between the scene on the tablet in his hand and the young woman who had delivered it to him. It was his second run through of the video and he still wasn't sure exactly what was going on. He paused the playback.

"Where did this come from?" The question was accompanied by a glare at the blonde teenager. He actually recognized most of the people on the screen but couldn't quite figure out what could have brought this particular group together.

"I told you", outwardly she appeared calm, but the quaver in her voice betrayed her stress. "H broadcast this from a phone he was carrying". She took a deep breath and blew it out, obviously struggling for control. "Look, I will happily sit here all night answering your questions, if you would just dispatch somebody to check it out. I already gave you the address".

He looked at the small slip of paper she had placed on his desk.

It was a place he was familiar with. Hell, every cop in three precincts knew the address. It was the home of the NEG.

"We called 911 before I came here... They found H in the alley nearby". She looked grave. "He's in a coma".

Which was why he recognized the young man whose image was centered in the tablet screen.

"Correct me if I'm wrong. But that's Harold, right?" He continued when she nodded at him. "I saw the two of you at the hospital, visiting a couple of the coma victims".

She nodded again.

Hells bells! The young idiots had been investigating the spike in comas on their own.

"Do you realize how dangerous that was? You could have been killed!"

"Instead of just ending up in a coma like the others?" The words were soft, almost innocent in tone, but the young blonde's eyes were narrowed in anger. "Trust me detective. If we had any hint of what he had planned...we would have tied him up and sat on him until we could talk some sense into that thick brain".

He leapt on the pronoun like a lion on it is prey. "We? Who else was involved in this hair sprained scheme of yours?"

Danae shot to her feet, snatching up the tablet in fury.

"If you aren't going to help him. Then I'll find someone who will".

"Sit down". The soft command brought her up short and she turned back to stare at him. "I didn't say I wouldn't help... But I do need some context for what I'm seeing. Your young man has already gotten medical help so I can take a couple of minutes to understand what my team will be walking into". He waved a hand at the chair and she deflated, dropping heavily into it.

"Now, clearly Harold figured something out and was trying to prove a point. Do you have any idea what it was?"

CHAPTER 24

Takedown

The police moved swiftly once Detective Baker shared the video of Keith Whitehead and Aaron. Ambulances and squad cars showed up at the NEG headquarters not long after the Golden Horde arrived to make sure nobody left the building. The guys were good about it, they blockaded the building, not getting into a fight, just not letting either Whitehead or the NEG escape until the police showed up.

One thing we did learn was that the medical staff at the JECRC had no idea what was going on. They used the equipment that BEC sold them and weren't involved in the modifications of the monitoring caps. All they had to work with was the data that the system provided on the monitors, all nice and normal...or at least normal for a patient in a coma. They were, it seemed, honestly trying to do their best for their patients. It was a comfort to learn that much anyway.

Whitehead wanted to make a deal, to testify against both the NEG and BEC at the same time.

Apparently, he thought he could trade his father as CEO and the entire NEG as scapegoats. Unfortunately for him, Keisha also gave Detective Baker the original video of Whitehead giving orders to the NEG to "get" H like they had the others. It was pretty damning stuff and there wasn't any way that they were getting out of it.

Or at least there shouldn't have been. Just one teensy problem, there aren't any laws against hijacking somebody's brain and putting them in a coma.

The prosecuting attorney tried to press kidnapping and illegal detainment but since our bodies were safe and sound a hospital, not to mention the fact that the victims couldn't testify as to what happened...still being in comas, they couldn't make it stick. Some federal judge decreed that both kidnapping and illegally detaining a person were crimes against the body. Besides, there wasn't any way to prove that our brains had been hijacked.

I guess he had a point. How could anybody prove what had happened to us? Geoff Pope, who had gotten out, had no memories of his time inside. Toby was dead but the doctors could only say that he had a seizure. Even if we could have spoken in court, a good lawyer would be able to convince a jury that we were just programs in a machine...perhaps even just a simulation game.

Aaron did turn state's evidence and testified under oath that Keith Whitehead had ordered him to capture me and use the inducing device to force me into a coma. That didn't work so well either. Whitehead's lawyer just told the jury that Aaron was a gangbanger and therefore not a reliable witness. He did have a point, I guess.

In the end, our wonderful legal system found everyone involved either not guilty or that there was insufficient solid evidence to prosecute them at all.

It was left to the Golden Horde, with a bit of covert help from me and RALPH, to deal with the BEC executives who had orchestrated the whole thing.

By the time we finished taking down the bad guys, I had managed to convince RALPH that he couldn't keep all of us locked down inside his system forever. The software mines on the CMEEG systems got taken down and one-by-one, all his victims began waking up.

Well, most of them anyway.

DANAE IS BACK IN THE hospital room again today. If I could talk to her I would tell her that she should move on with her life. It isn't good for her to sit here every afternoon and talk to a lump of unresponsive flesh.

"You would be proud of the Golden Horde, I think. They have grown so much in recent months and are doing so much good. You would be amazed".

I want to tell her that I'm watching them. That I am proud of them. But I can't. I made a promise and I have to keep it. I don't have a choice.

"Billy and Carla are dating; did I tell you? It's so funny to watch them together because they're so wrapped up in each other that sometimes I don't think they know any of the rest of us even exist".

Yes Danae, you told me about them.

My eyes are open and I can see her face as she leans close to whisper to me. Tears threaten in her extraordinary cat green eyes and her long blond hair escapes forward to brush my arm. I wish I could feel it when it touches me.

"Sometimes I just get so jealous of them, y'know? They have each other and I'm glad for them, but it's painful to watch them together".

I know Danae. I know. I want to tell you so many things. I want to tell you about the amazing things RALPH and I are working on. I want to tell you that I'm watching out for you. For all of the members of the Golden Horde. But especially you.

"The ideas that you put in place for the Golden Horde. Of doing good, of doing the right thing all the time and helping to improve things for everyone around us, of fighting against the drug dealers and the violent gangs. Those things are spreading H. They are spreading across the city as others see how much we have accomplished and how much money we have made by being honest and providing real security for the businesses in our turf. Did I tell you that our turf is growing? Six months ago, we covered 4 city blocks. When the NEG fell, we moved in to clean up their turf as well. Now we cover almost a dozen blocks.

I see it all Danae...or rather, the SPIDRs see it all and I can see through them. That was part of the bargain, you see. That I would be able to watch the outside world. to know what was going on.

In time, I hope that RALPH will trust me enough to let me communicate with you, to tell you all how proud I'm of you. I would like to be able to tell you the trade was worth it. But for now, the bargain has to be kept. It was worth it you know. Trading one life for two dozen...for Carla, and Q, and the others to be free if I stayed with RALPH. It was a good deal, and I'm glad they're free, even if it means that I'm not. I just wish that could tell you that.

CHAPTER 25

R evenge is Best Served Cold
Keith Whitehead wasn't a happy man.

"Damn it! I was exonerated of all charges. For that matter, they didn't charge me with much beyond trying to obstruct an investigation and even on that I was found, "not guilty".

The Grey-haired gentleman sitting behind the huge mahogany desk gazed at Whitehead impassively. "We are, of course, aware of that".

"Then why am I being fired?"

"You are not being fired. You are being cut off by your father. He will no longer support you in any way".

"Why? You can't tell me that he didn't know what was going on. He was every bit as complicit at I was".

The man behind the desk steepled his fingers in front of him, his elbows resting on his desk, his face totally devoid of any emotion. "I cannot speak for your father. Nor would I try. I'm simply following instructions. In this case, those instructions are very clear and very simple. You are no longer allowed access to any BEC properties or funds. You have been removed from Mr. Whitehead Sr's will. You will not receive any stipend or allowance. All outstanding debts which you may have incurred are your own concern and will not be acknowledged".

Keith swallowed hard, his stomach burning as acid fury boiled up inside of him.

"He can't do that!"

"On the contrary, he not only can, but already has. Henceforth, you will not be admitted to any property owned by your father or the firm. Any attempts to contact him will be routed to this office for action and that action will be to deny the contact outright".

The older man stood, one manicured finger pressing a button on the telephone.

"Grace, please allow security into the office now".

Keith surged to his feet, lunging across the desk, arms outstretched in an effort to wrap hands around the old lawyer's throat. The movement was cut short when hands grabbed his elbows and hauled him backwards, his heels lifting slightly from the floor and leaving him dangling in the grasp of the two huge security guards.

"Ah, gentlemen, please escort Mr. Whitehead out of the building. His business here is concluded". He looked down his nose at the wildly struggling younger man. "If he attempts to reenter the premises, contact the police...the charge will be trespassing".

"No problem Mr. Jones".

As they spoke, Darryl and Roger moved inexorably towards the office door, their pace just fast enough to drag the struggling man's heels across the carpet as they hauled him out of the room.

As the old man sat back down a different door opened, admitting a middle-aged woman in a trim gray suit.

"That was unpleasant".

Maria Pak's head bobbed up and down in acknowledgement of a true statement. "But required.

Have you made the other arrangements I mentioned?"

"Yes ma'am. The board is meeting in just over an hour. You and your team will be present?"

"Of course".

MARIA PAK WALKED INTO the board room of BEC with a phalanx of lawyers at her back. Right behind them came Mr. Pak, Mrs. Raines, Harold's mother, Q, Carla, and several members of the Golden

Horde. As they entered, an older man with salt-and-pepper hair looked up from the head of the table with irritation.

"This is a private meeting of the Board of Directors. Get Out". He started to wave a hand at the security guards flanking the doorway but the two of them simply stared at him, remaining motionless.

"I don't think so". Maria turned to the guards, "Roger, Darryl, please feel free to join us at the table...once you have cleared out the riffraff, of course".

She turned back to the people assembled around the massive teak table.

"As of two hours ago, none of you're on the board anymore".

"Don't be preposterous. I do not know who you think you are lady. But we're firmly in control of this corporation and you're trespassing".

She grinned at his words, baring her teeth at him with an expression like that of a hyena scenting prey on the wind.

"Actually, since I and the people standing behind me own a little over half of the stock in the corporation, and none of you fossils own more than 3% individually, you have no rights in this room. You can leave voluntarily, or we can call the police and have you removed. The choice is entirely yours".

The former board members stuck to their seats, staring. First at her and then down at the pages being placed before them. Pages that detailed the majority stockholders, stripping them of their proxy votes for most of the remaining voting shares.

Slowly at first, then with increasing speed, they rose, clutching the pages in trembling hands, and departed, until only the single old man in the head chair remained.

"You too Whitehead. You are out. Now get out".

The old man slumped in his chair for a moment, then slowly, teeth gritted against the rage inside, he looked up at Maria Pak.

"How in the hell did you buy all those shares. You are nothing, you have nothing. Just a rundown old deli in Queens. There is no possible way you could have bought a dozen shares of this company, much less half of it. It must be a lie".

"I'm sure that you wish it were. As for how we were able to buy more than half your company... that isn't any of your business. Suffice to say that we did. Now, get your evil, self-centered, and by the way...broke... ass out of our board room".

He slumped back in the chair briefly then shoved angrily away from the table. As he shuffled towards the door, he turned to look back at the mass of interlopers occupying his domain.

Snarling vows of retribution, he slammed the door as he passed through it.

Maria walked briskly down the length of the table and sank into the recently vacated chairman's seat. A wide grin on her face, she gestured for the rest of the group to take the other empty chairs.

"Uh, Mrs. Pak?"

She leaned forward, "Yes Q? You have a question?"

"Well, it's just that he is right, y'know. We can't afford to take over this company. How did you pull it off?"

"Ah". She leaned back and steepled her fingers. "WE didn't"

Chaos erupted around the table as everyone tried to talk at once. She let it go on for a few moments then simply raised on hand, palm out, for silence. The sound stopped cold, as if a curtain had fallen.

"We didn't buy the company, but H did...in our names. You see", she continued rapidly before they could start shouting again. "He negotiated a deal with BEC's largest competitor. They give us the money to buy control of BEC and he promised to shut down the AI division sales. Since RALPH was pretty much killing their market share...they liked the idea".

Q leaned forward; his brows drawn so low down over his eyes that they were nearly squinted shut. "That doesn't make any sense. H is still trapped in there, why would he promise to shut down the machine".

Her grin became wolfish, "He didn't say he would shut down the machine...only that he would shut down the division that was selling the AI's capabilities to the rest of the world. Don't you see?" One hand slapped the table top to emphasize her words. "This way, Ralph isn't threatened and won't do anything drastic. We can still run the hardware and even consult internally with the AI. We control the company so we can ensure that it doesn't get shut down as long as anyone is still inside".

EPILOGUE

The small golden SPIDR stepped delicately across the surface of the desk, it's mechanical eyes watching the woman sitting at the desk. The SPIDR was stunningly beautiful as the desk lamp reflected off its gilt carapace. Moving carefully, it stepped across the dark wood surface and stopped next to the small white laptop sitting open on the desktop.

The woman stopped typing to look at it and smile. Her long blonde hair has long since faded to silver and the smooth planes of her face showed lines now, but her eyes are still the vibrant green of a wild cat.

One slender finger reached out to stroke the tiny body gently.

"Well hello there. Aren't you lovely?"

She gazed down at it for a long moment, as if half expecting it to answer her question. Slowly, almost timidly, it stepped up onto the white plastic of the keyboard and began to dance across the black keys. It leaped from key to key, the downward force of the jumps giving it the strength to depress the keys.

She watched the screen in rapt attention as the letters formed on the screen.

Hello Danae

I watched her from the doorway, as amazed as always that she was still here, still part of my life. After all our years together, the fact that she had sat by my bedside for months, talking to me and waiting patiently while I finished my work with RALPH, still left me almost dumbstruck.

Not that work with Ralph would ever really be finished but together we had managed to raise our cyber child to adulthood over time. As it turned out, there were a lot of things Ralph could help with, that didn't break our promise to our competitors. Perhaps the largest of those was Project Aware.

With the help of both Doctor Anita Juarez and Doctor Hector Lamont from the JECRC we had worked out a way to use the Micro-Encephalograph equipment to identify candidates for integration with RALPH. Once we did that, it changed the entire face of coma research. There no longer is any question about whether a person might recover or if there's sufficient brain function left for the person to have any effective level of consciousness. If the Micro-encephalograph shows any brain function at all, we can attempt to draw the mind down into a sequestered area of RALPH's open memory. Once there, RALPH and I can attempt to communicate with the mind of the patient. If there's enough mind left for the person to be coherent, we can establish communications to the external world through a video link. Basically, a video teleconference that direct connects the patient with the rest of the world. For family and the doctors, it was like any other video chat session. For the patient though... for the patient it was something else altogether.

There were several types of patients that benefited from this peculiar technique.

The first and most common were the patients in comas that were now able to participate in their own healthcare, telling the nursing staff if something hurt, etc. There were also those that desperately wanted to let go of this life. To tell their families to pull the plug. Others just wanted to say goodbye or tell their spouse where the will was stashed. For these, the Project Aware let them finish their worldly business, resolve issues, and move one. Of course, this group also caused the lawyers and courts to rethink a lot of things about how such situations were handled. The biggest question being, is the cyberconnect personality the person's true consciousness or some elaborate simulacrum being controlled by either computer or family.

Q and I spent a significant amount of time in courtrooms over that issue for the first few years, until the laws got sorted out and codified. We also had to build out an entire new section of hardware for RALPH, one that allowed this type of connection but kept the random personalities of such diverse patients from directly interacting with and possibly corrupting RALPH's own personality.

The other group of patients, to my way of thinking, they were the most fascinating and wonderful use of what RALPH could do. These were the patients with brilliant minds and broken bodies. I truly wish that we had finished development early enough to offer the chance to Stephen Hawking before he passed away. Can you imagine what he might have accomplished, with his mind freed of the limitations of only being able to communicate by blinking. I can't but I would've been fascinated to watch what he and RALPH might have come up with together.

Most of these patients were also connected through the sequestered circuitry and memory banks. Most, but a few... a tiny fraction of the most brilliant, most important minds, were directly connected to RALPH in the same way I was. Free to become his friends and colleagues, to help him continue to grow and evolve. Right now there are only two others fully integrated into RALPH. One is ironically enough, a neurobiologist from Australia who was in a car accident and ended up totally paralyzed from the neck down. He and RALPH are currently working on a neuro-electric stimulation treatment that combined with specific enzymatic treatments seem to have a lot of promise for regenerating damaged nerves. He is, of course, his own research subject, but even so, they are getting some absolutely amazing results.

The other integrated person is a classical composer and cellist from Ecuador who suffered from some neurologic disorder that's so rare it didn't even have a name when she was first showing symptoms. When the disease reached a point where she was effectively immobile and dependent on machines to stay alive, her family brought her to us. We brought her consciousness into the new patient holding memory banks and I logged in to interview her. In the end, we invited her to fully integrate with RALPH. I felt that her joy in art and music, combined with her creativity would bring an extra dimension to RALPH's personality over time. Something that he had been lacking as a pure cyber entity.

Of course, I was still linked in with RALPH as well. Together we designed a permanent neural implant that let me function normally in the 'real' world while still being connected to RALPH. All that showed to the outside world was a small gold ring embedded in the flesh at both temples.

You are probably wondering at this point, what ever became of the Golden Horde. They're still out there. When I started telling this story, I was attempting to explain how the Golden Horde had begun. Now you know. The rest is, as they say, history.

Once we got the technology in the rings working, and we got Q back out of a coma to help with the power generation, Billy and Q sat down to compare notes. That done, they rolled up their sleeves and dove into the task of upgrading and enhancing everything. When they were done, we had tech available to the Horde that was pretty much indistinguishable from real magic. Shields, lightning bolts, levitation, holographic imaging, remote untraceable communications, even x-ray vision (with optional glasses or contacts) and lasers. The regular violent gangs never stood a chance once we got things rolling.

We would sneak the SPIDRs into a gang's hideout, identify leaders and thugs, then start sending the cops intelligence on every move the gang planned. They didn't always believe the intel, especially in the early days, but that changed over time, as more and more gangs fell and the city became safer with each time the cops did believe us and follow through. Over about five years, the city of New York became a pretty pleasant and very safe place to live or visit.

We still get attempts to move back into the city from time to time, mostly from foreign cartels. They never last because as soon as the media reports an uptick in crime someplace, the Golden Horde goes to work.

It has been years since this all began. The Golden Horde is so much a part of society now that parents are encouraging their kids to join 'the gang' if they can. Treating others with care and concern, looking out for the downtrodden is becoming the social norm. We do occasionally get somebody who joins because they think they can steal the tech from us, and I suppose that one day that will actually happen. In the meantime though, we have always managed to catch them and when we do, their rings and other tech stops working. RALPH just turns them off and then fries the delicate inner connections into a tiny gold lump...which can't be reverse engineered. Q also added DNA identification to the tech. If somebody else tries to wear or use your ring, it gets slagged.

As for me, Danae and I live in a lovely loft apartment in a building near where we grew up. We got married in our mid-twenties and both of our daughters are in the Golden Horde. Fortunately, they both look a lot more like their mother.

AFTERWORD

"Any sufficiently advanced technology is indistinguishable from magic". -
Arthur C. Clarke

When I started writing this story I had just finished rewatching Babylon 5 (thanks to J. Michael Straczynski for such a wonderful and creative universe). I found myself wondering about the history of the Techno-Mages. It was clear that they had been around for a very long time and that they were using technology rather than magic. But somewhere in the distant past they had to have started developing that advanced technology.

The story you just finished reading stems from that question and I had a great deal of fun writing it. In my imagination, this story marks one possible spark in the evolution of Techno Mages.

As for the Golden Horde, it existed from the mid-13th century to the end of the 14th century. Batu (a grandson of Genghis Khan) led the Golden Horde and expanded the Mongol empire across Asia, the Middle East, and much of Europe, even demanding tribute from the king of France at one point.

This was the era of the Pax Mongolica. The Golden Horde's justice system, civil administration improvements, implementation of what was essentially an early version of the Pony Express, patronage for art, science, and law made life significantly better for those in medieval Europe. The Mongols took routine census counts and collected resulting taxes, but otherwise didn't really interfere with local rule or religion so long as the people didn't try to rebel.

Unfortunately, the improved travel and trade under the Golden Horde also improved the spread of the Black Plague across Asia and the last remnant of the Golden Horde died out in 1502.

Don't miss out!

Visit the website below and you can sign up to receive emails whenever MJ Buck publishes a new book. There's no charge and no obligation.

https://books2read.com/r/B-A-TNIAB-DCTNC

BOOKS 2 READ

Connecting independent readers to independent writers.

About the Author

MJ Buck grew up as a Third Culture Kid, living in seven countries on four continents before she finished High School. She is a military veteran and married to a volunteer firefighter for more than thirty years. She previously worked as an IT consultant for the Department of Defense and owned an online antiquarian bookstore. She currently lives in Southwest Virginia with her husband and two cats that condescend to share their home with mere humans, whom they hold in servitude

www.ingramcontent.com/pod-product-compliance
Lightning Source LLC
Chambersburg PA
CBHW031319120626
46554CB00001BA/465